King of the Wind

by
MARGUERITE HENRY

Cover illustration by Josef Hozak

Inside illustrations by Wesley Dennis

SCHOLASTIC INC.
New York Toronto London Auckland Sydney

Books by Marguerite Henry

Brighty of the Grand Canyon
Justin Morgan Had a Horse
King of the Wind
Misty of Chincoteague
Sea Star

ISBN 0-590-03050-7

14 13 12 11 10   9/8 0/9

Printed in the U.S.A.   11

To
SAMUEL RIDDLE
Owner of Man o' War

and

MELVILLE CHURCH II
*President, The Virginia Horseman's Association
in whose Thoroughbreds flows the blood
of the Godolphin Arabian*

CONTENTS

THE GREAT SON

T HE MORNING FOG HAD LIFTED, giving way to a clear day. Nearly all the people of Windsor, Ontario, and thousands of visitors were surging into Kenilworth Park, filling the stands and overflowing to the infield. It was the greatest crowd ever to attend a race in Canada. For this was the day of the match race between Man o' War, the great American horse, and Sir Barton, the pride of Canada.

Bands were playing, first an American air, then a Canadian air. Flags of both countries draped the grandstand and fluttered against the sky.

Under a covered paddock Man o' War, affection-
ately known as Big Red, was being saddled for his
twenty-first race. As the trainer was about to tighten
the girth strap, he turned to the jockey at his elbow.
"Let Red run his own race," he said. "Don't hold
him in."

The freckle-faced jockey nodded. He looked
over at the clock. In exactly twenty minutes Man o'
War would meet Sir Barton, the horse that had
won the Kentucky Derby, the Preakness, the Bel-
mont, in one year. Sir Barton was a Triple Crown
champion, a horse to be reckoned with!

The trainer finished his careful check of saddle-
cloths and weight pads, and signaled to the jockey,
who swung up on Man o' War. He had ten minutes
to walk him around the saddling ring, ten minutes
to calm him down. Without this ritual, Big Red was
as unruly as a colt.

Across the paddock the trainer caught the eye
of Samuel Riddle, owner of Man o' War. They
watched the ripple of the smooth muscles as the
horse walked, the curving of his powerful neck, the
burnished red-gold of his coat. Their glances
locked. "Big Red's in fine fettle," they were agree-
ing with each other. "He's in top form."

Meanwhile, in Sir Barton's camp, well-laid plans

8

were being rehearsed. Sir Barton was to run an explosion race. Instead of matching speed for speed around the track, he was to start off with a wild spurt and run Man o' War off his feet. It was a good plan, for everyone knew there was no greater sprinter than Sir Barton. If, at the very start of the race, he could get Man o' War to overreach his usual stride, he might never find it again. The race could be won in the first furlong.

The bugle sounded. Sir Barton, a dark chestnut horse, and Man o' War, the red-gold stallion, were paraded past the judges' stand, past the grandstand, past the stand where moving-picture men were grinding their cameras. Man o' War heard the roar of the crowds. He smelled his opponent. But his eyes were fixed on the track, spread out clean and inviting before him. He knew what it meant. Business! *His* business. Racing! He had walked enough. He was ready to go!

Now he was moving toward the barrier, plunging against it nervously, trying to spring it. Sir Barton caught his excitement. He strained against the webbing. And almost at once it was sprung.

Like a two-horse team the golden-red horse and the dark chestnut were off together. According to plan, Sir Barton's jockey began using the whip, and

9

the Canadian horse shot to the front in one of the fastest sprints in history.

Man o' War's jockey was holding him back, saving speed for the finish. But Man o' War had other ideas. He fought for his head. He pulled at the bit. He was in business for himself!

And then the jockey remembered the trainer's words: "Let Red run his own race. Don't hold him in." He gave Man o' War his head. Like a dynamo on the loose, Big Red leaped out. He was a machine with pistons for legs, pistons that struck out in perfect rhythm. He caught Sir Barton. He flew past him in great long leaps.

It was Man o' War who was running the explosion race. It was Man o' War who was running Sir Barton off his feet!

The jockey looked back. He saw the Canadian horse hopelessly trying to recover his own pace. The race was as good as won. It *was* won! Man o' War passed the finish post seven lengths ahead.

The crowds swept onto the track, throwing walking sticks, hats, handkerchiefs, high in the air. They forgot whether they were Canadians or Americans. They had never seen a race like this. They surged toward the judges' platform where Man o' War was standing proudly by, while Samuel Riddle was accepting the gold trophy cup that the big horse had won.

"Your horse can't be beaten!" Sir Barton's owner exclaimed as he shook Mr. Riddle's hand.

Suddenly Big Red shied. He had heard the popping of the cork of a champagne bottle. Then his curiosity overcame him. He nosed closer, watching as the wine bubbled into the trophy cup. He was thirsty. He strained toward the cup. Mr. Riddle smiled.

"Bring me some water that is not too cold," he directed.

While the crowd murmured in surprise, Mr. Riddle poured the champagne out on the turf. He wiped the cup with a clean handkerchief. Then he filled it with water. He held it toward the horse, and Man o' War drank out of the great gold cup.

"He won it, didn't he?" Mr. Riddle asked, his voice strangely husky.

A cheer went up from thirty thousand throats. It was a good ending to a good race!

Sir Barton's owner was right. Big Red could *not* be beaten. Already the three-year-old colt had made five American records and two world records. He had proved himself a terrific sprinter over short distances and a powerful stayer over long ones.

11

Even more remarkable, he had carried a handicap of more than 130 pounds, while his rivals carried 114 pounds, 108 pounds, 104 pounds.

No wonder the crowds took this great colt to their hearts! There was no telling what the future held in store for him.

Friends had urged Mr. Riddle to send Man o' War to England after the Windsor race. They wanted him to run in the famous Newmarket races, where his great ancestors had run. A victory at Newmarket would mean more to Big Red's admirers than all his smashing victories in America. For they had experienced a deep hurt when their favorite horse was excluded from the British Stud Book because he was not all Thoroughbred. To have him win at Newmarket would ease the hurt.

But Big Red was never to race again. Mr. Riddle had come to a most important decision. On a night not long before the race in Canada, he had visited in New York with the judge who determined how much weight each horse should carry to make a race evenly matched.

"Man o' War will soon be a four-year-old," Mr. Riddle said. "What weight will you give him then?"

The reply came without hesitation. "I'll have to give him more weight than ever a race horse carried," the judge said. "Man o' War is the greatest horse alive."

Samuel Riddle knew Man o' War was so strong and swift that he had to carry more weight than other horses. He accepted the decision as fair. But he knew, too, that more weight might weaken Man o' War's legs, might break his great fighting heart as well. It would be better to retire him in perfect condition, without a mark on him. Mr. Riddle made up his mind. After the match race with Sir Barton, he would withdraw Big Red from racing.

Telling no one of his decision, he masked his sorrow in silence. Neither his trainer, nor his jockey, nor Man o' War's thousands of friends at the Canadian race suspected the truth. Alone, in that crowd of thirty thousand, Mr. Riddle knew that he was watching Big Red run his last race.

When the roar and the tumult were over, he quietly gave out the news. Followers of Big Red were stunned. After Newmarket it would have seemed all right to retire Man o' War. His victory there would have been a fitting ending post to a great career. But now . . .

Friends, and strangers too, tried to persuade Man o' War's owner to change his mind.

Mr. Riddle only smiled in that quiet way of his.

13

He knew that Big Red did not need victories at Newmarket to prove his pedigree. What did it matter if one of his great-great-granddams was a carthorse and had less than royal blood in her veins? What did it matter that she had kept him out of the *Who's Who* of the horse world? In male descent, Man o' War's blood was traceable in unbroken line to the great Godolphin Arabian himself!

And then Mr. Riddle began to think about the Godolphin Arabian. He had not raced at Newmarket either. And he had no pedigree at all. It had been lost. He had to write a new one with his own blood — the blood that flowed in the veins of his sons and daughters.

Man o' War could do that too. The great son could follow in the footsteps of his famous ancestor. He could live on in his colts and grandcolts. They could win the races at Newmarket.

But it was not easy for Mr. Riddle to convince his friends that this plan was the right one. Often he had to go back two hundred years and tell them the story of the Godolphin Arabian.

THE FAST OF RAMADAN

IN THE NORTHWESTERN SLICE OF AFRICA known as
Morocco, a horseboy stood with broom in hand
in the vast courtyard of the royal stables of the Sultan. He was waiting for dusk to fall.

All day long he had eaten nothing. He had not
even tasted the jujubes tucked in his turban, nor
the enormous purple grapes that spilled over the

palace wall into the stable yard. He had tried not to sniff the rich, warm fragrance of ripening pomegranates. For this was the sacred month of Ramadan when, day after day, all faithful Mohammedans neither eat nor drink from the dawn before sunrise until the moment after sunset.

The boy Agba had not minded the fast for himself. It was part of his religion. But when Signor Achmet, Chief of the Grooms, commanded that the horses too observe the fast, Agba's dark eyes smouldered with anger.

"It is the order of the Sultan!" the Signor had announced to the horseboys. And he had cuffed Agba on the head when the boy showed his disapproval.

Of the twelve thousand horses in the Sultan's stables, Agba had charge of ten. He fed and watered them and polished their coats and cleaned their stalls. Best of all, he wheeled the whole string into the courtyard at one time for their exercise.

There was one of the ten horses to whom Agba had lost his heart. She was a bay mare, as fleet as a gazelle, with eyes that studied him in whatever he did. The other nine horses he would lead out to the common water trough to drink. But for his bright bay he would fill a water cask from a pure spring

16

beyond the palace gates. Then he would hold it while the mare sucked the water, her eyelashes brushing his fingers as she drank. For long moments after she had drunk her fill, she would gaze at him while the cool water dribbled from her muzzle onto his hands.

It was the mare that worried Agba now as he worked to fill in the time until the hour of sunset. The courtyard was already swept clean, but Agba pushed his palm-leaf broom as if he were sweeping all his thoughts into a little mound for the wind to carry away.

At last he hung his broom on an iron hook alongside an endless row of brooms and went to the mare. Her stall door was closed, so that the fragrance of late clover would not drift in to prick her appetite. He found her asleep, lying on her side, her great belly distended by the little colt soon to be born. Agba noticed, with a heavy feeling in his chest, that the fast was telling on the mare. He could read it in the sunken places above each eye, in the harshness of her coat.

But soon the fast would be over. It was the last day of the month, and even now the sun was sinking below the gray-green olive trees that fringed the courtyard.

There was no sound anywhere, not from the palace walls beyond, nor from the quarters over the stables where the horseboys lived. The whole world seemed to be holding its breath, waiting for dusk to fall. Small voices of insects and birds were beginning to pierce the quiet. Twilight toads piping on their bassoons. Crickets chirping. Wood doves cooing. And afar off in the Atlas Mountains a hyena began to laugh. These were forerunners of the darkness. It would be only a short time now.

Agba turned toward the east, his eyes on the minaret of the mosque. It was a sharp needle pricking the blood-red reflection of the sun. He gazed fixedly at it until his eyes smarted. At last a figure in white robes emerged from the tower. It was the public crier. He was sounding his trumpet. He was crying four times to the four winds of heaven. The fast of Ramadan was at an end!

The air went wild with noise. Twelve thousand horses recognized the summons and neighed their hunger. The royal stables seethed like an ant hill. Horseboys swarmed out of the corridors and into the courtyard. From the hoods of their cloaks, from waistbands and vests, they took dates and raisins and almonds and popped them noisily into their mouths. They stripped the grapes from their vines. They ate with boisterous abandon. Some plunged their faces into the troughs and sucked the water as if they were horses.

Agba did not join the other horseboys. He returned to the mare. Moving slowly so as not to frighten her, he reached under the saddle hung on the wall and found the water vessel he had filled and hidden there an hour ago. He poured the water into a basin and waited for the mare to awaken.

As if she had heard in her dreams the sound made by the water, she woke with a jerk and struggled to her feet. She came to Agba and drank. Then she raised her head, letting the water slobber from her lips.

Agba waited motionless, knowing she would want more and more. Her deep brown eyes studied him as if to say, "You are the source of all that is good."

A great happiness welled up inside Agba. He nodded, seeming to understand her thoughts, then waited while she drank again and again.

When Agba came out of the mare's stall, the other boys were beginning to lead their horses to the common trough to drink. He must hurry now if he hoped to get his corn ration first. He picked up a bag made of hemp and ran through a maze of corridors and down a steep staircase to the underground granary. At the entrance stood Signor Achmet, Chief of the Grooms. Signor Achmet was dark and bearded. In his right hand he carried a knotted stick, and from the sash at his waist hung a hundred keys. When he saw Agba, he gripped the boy's shoulder with fingers as strong as the claws of an eagle.

"Why do you not eat with the other slaveboys?" he asked in his cracked voice. Then with a sharp look he released Agba and began peeling an orange with his fingernails. His beady eyes did not leave Agba's face as he ate the orange, making loud sucking noises to show how juicy and good it was.

Agba gulped. He studied his brown toes.

"Is it the mare?"

The boy's eyes flew to the Signor's.

"Is tonight her hour?"

Slowly, gravely, Agba nodded.

"Tonight, then," the Signor said, as he wiped his mouth on his mantle and began fumbling for the key to the granary, "tonight you will not go to your quarters to sleep. You will move the mare into the brood-mare stable. You will remain on watch and call me when she is ready to foal. The all-seeing eye of Allah will be upon you."

Agba's heart fluttered like bird wings. The Chief of the Grooms was letting him stay with his mare! He forgot all the cuffs and sharp words. He bowed low, impatient to hear the sound of the key turning the great lock, impatient for the creaking of the door and the mingled odors of corn and barley.

The key scraped. The door creaked open. The warm, mellow smells leaked out.

Signor Achmet stood aside. Agba slipped past him into the darkness. Quickly his sensitive fingers sought the good, sound ears of corn. He filled his bag with them. Then he turned and fled up the stairs.

THE BROOD-MARE STABLE

Bᵁᵀ ᵀᴴᴱ ᴹᴬᴿᴱ ᵂᴼᵁᴸᴰ ᴺᴼᵀ ᴱᴬᵀ the corn Agba
brought. She only lipped it, then closed her
eyes with a great weariness.

Agba was troubled as he watered and fed the
other horses in his aisle, as he ate his own meal of
barley and goat's milk, as he hurried to the brood-
mare stable.

Signor Achmet must have been there before him. One of the stalls was wide open, and a lanthorn hung on a peg, sending out a feeble light. The stall had not been used since spring, and had a fusty smell. Agba leaped upon the manger and threw open a tiny round window. It showed a patch of sky and the new moon.

"This is a favorable sign," he thought. "A new moon. A new month. The foal will be strong and swift." He took a deep breath of the cool summer night. Then quickly he went to work, filling bucket after bucket of sand from the huge sand pile behind the stables. Back and forth he ran, dumping the sand on the floor of the stall. Next he covered it with straw, spreading it out first with his hands, then trotting over it, galloping over it, around and around. At last he surveyed his work with approval. It would be a good bed for the mare!

Just as he was filling the manger with fodder, Signor Achmet, in flowing white robes, looked in. He tested the depth of the sand with a bony fore-finger. He felt the straw.

"You waste the sand and the straw," he said with a black look. "Half would do." But the Signor understood Agba's concern for the mare. "Fetch her now," he commanded.

Agba's bow was lost in the darkness.

"You will summon me when she grows restless."

Swiftly and silently the Signor turned upon his heel, his white mantle fluttering behind him like moth wings.

The new moon hung over Agba's shoulder as he ran to get the mare. She was standing patiently in a corner of her stall, her head lowered, her tail tucked in. Placing a hand on her neck, Agba led her out into the night, past endless stalls and under endless archways to her new quarters. She walked slowly, heavily.

At the door of the new stall a tremor of fear shook her. She made a feeble attempt to go back, but Agba held her firmly, humming to hide his own nameless fears.

She entered the stall. She tried the soft bed with her feet. She went to the manger. Her nostrils widened to snuff the dried grasses, but she did not eat. She put her lips to the water cask, but did not drink. At last she tucked her hooves underneath her and with a groan lay down. Her head nodded. She steadied it in the straw. Then her breathing, too, steadied.

As Agba stood on watch, his mind was a mill wheel, turning, turning, turning. He trembled, remembering the time he and the mare had come upon a gazelle, and he had ridden the mare alongside the gazelle, and she had outrun the wild thing. Agba could still feel the wind singing in his ears.

By closing his eyes, he brought back the whole day. On the way home they had passed a wizened old storyteller in the streets, who, when Agba came near, motioned him close. The old man placed his hand on the mare's head. Then, in a voice that was no more than a whisper, he had said, "When Allah created the horse, he said to the wind, 'I will that a creature proceed from thee. Condense thyself.' And the wind condensed itself, and the result was the horse."

The words danced in Agba's head as he watched the sleeping mare. *I will that a creature proceed from thee. Condense thyself! I will that a creature proceed from thee. Condense thyself!* He told the words over and over in his mind, until suddenly the stable walls faded away and Agba was riding the South Wind. And there was nothing to stop him. No palace walls. No trees. Nor hedges. Nor rivers. Only white clouds to ride through, and a blue vaulted archway, and the wind for a mount.

With a sigh he sank down in the straw. His head dropped.

A FOAL IS BORN

THE BOY'S DREAMS SPUN THEMSELVES OUT until there was nothing left of them. He slept a deep sleep. The candle in the lanthorn sputtered and died. The new moon rode higher and higher. Bats and nighthawks, flying noiselessly in the velvet night, went about their business, swooping insects out of the air. With the gray light of morning they vanished, giving way to the jangling chorus of the crows.

Agba woke. The stable walls had closed in again. And there was the mare lying on her side as before. But her head was raised now, and she was drying off a newborn foal! Her tongue strokes filled the silence of the stall, licking, licking, licking.

The boy watched in fear that if he took his eyes away the whole scene might vanish into the mist of the morning. Oh, how tiny the foal was! And so wet there was no telling what its color would be. But its eyes were open. And they were full of curiosity.

Agba's body quivered with the wonder of the little fellow's birth. He had seen newborn foals before, but none so small and finely made. In the distance he could hear the softly padding feet of the horseboys. He could hear the wild boar grunting and coughing in his hole behind the stables. He wondered if the boar really did keep evil spirits from entering into the horses.

Afraid to move, he watched the mare clumsily get to her feet. He watched her nudge the young thing with her nose.

The foal tried to get up. He thrust out his forefeet, but they splayed and he seemed to get all tangled up with himself. He tried again and again. For one breathless instant he was on his feet. Then his legs buckled and he fell in a little heap. Agba reached a hand toward him, but the mare came between. She pushed the little one with her nose. She pushed him with her tongue. She nickered to him. He was trying again. He was standing up. How spindly he was! And his ribs showed. And he had hollows above his eyes, just like his dam.

"I could carry him in my arms," thought Agba. "He is not much bigger than a goat, and he has long whiskers like a goat. Long and silky. And his tail is curly. And he is all of one color. Except — except . . ." Suddenly the boy's heart missed a beat. On the off hind heel there was a white spot. It was no bigger than an almond, but it was there! The white spot — the emblem of swiftness!

Agba leaped to his feet. He wanted to climb the tower of the mosque. He wanted to blow on the trumpet. He wanted to cry to the four winds of heaven: "A foal is born! And he will be swift as the wind of the desert, for on his hind heel is a white spot. A white spot. A white . . ."

Just then a shaft of early sunlight pierced the

window of the stable and found the colt. It flamed his coat into red-gold. It made a sun halo around his head.

Agba was full of fear. He opened his mouth, but no sound escaped. Maybe this was all a dream. Maybe the foal was not real. The golden coat. The crown of sun rays. Maybe he was a golden horse belonging to the chariot of the sun!

"I'll capture him with a name," the boy thought quickly. And he named the young thing Sham, which is the Arabic word for sun.

No sooner had Agba fastened a name on him than the little creature seemed to take on a new strength. He took a few steps. He found his mother's milk. He began to nurse, making soft sucking noises.

Agba knew he should be reporting to Signor Achmet. He knew he should be standing in line for his measure of corn. But he could not bear to break the spell. He listened to the colt suckling, to the mare munching the dried grasses. He smelled their warm bodies. A stable was a *good* place to be born.

THE WHEAT EAR

A GBA'S THOUGHTS WERE BROUGHT UP SHARPLY. The door to the stall was opening silently, and Signor Achmet was standing over him, the sun glinting along his saber. An angry light leaped into his eyes as he looked down at the boy.

Agba sprang to his feet, waiting for the tongue-lashing, waiting for the bony fingers on his shoulder.

30

Agba ran out of the stall. He took no more notice of the boys in the corridors than if they had been flies. He did not know where he was going. He only knew that he wanted to run until he could run no more — away from death and life.

He ran now, down through the wilderness of corridors to the courtyard gate. Two soldiers were patrolling the gate. They waved Agba through without question. Was he not the first slaveboy of Signor Achmet? Was he not often sent to the shops on errands for the chief groom?

"Run, run!" the soldiers cried to him.

Out the gates, down the hill to the city of Meknes he ran, past corn mills, past camels browsing before the tents of Arabs, past mules laden with crates of screaming chickens, past shepherds leading their flocks to market — down into the dark, crooked streets of the city. He ran faster and faster, dodging barking dogs and pigs and goats. He flew past the shops — the scriveners, the meat fryers, the shoemakers, the waxhandlers. Shopkeepers tried to stop him, to lay hold of his sash, but he was quicksilver in their hands.

"Some evil spirit must be after him," they laughed to each other, white teeth flashing.

33

On and on he went, weaving his way between street jugglers, snake charmers, water carriers, and small boys scurrying about with great trays of bread. He was trying to run away from trouble, but it hugged him like his own shadow. "Maybe if I run faster," he thought. He doubled his fists close to his body. He plunged on. He could feel his lungs pumping for air. His breath came so fast it hurt him. And suddenly he was almost knocked flat by the saddle trappings of a camel.

He stopped and stared. The camel was followed by her calf. A thought startled Agba. *Camel's milk!* Horses of the desert were often raised on it. He had heard Signor Achmet say it was better than mare's milk. Stronger. Richer.

He ran to the driver, pulling the hem of his mantle to attract his attention. The driver turned around angrily. At once he recognized Agba. The boy had often been sent to him to buy camel skins for making stirrup leathers.

The driver's scowl turned into a greedy smile. Here was an emissary from the royal stables, from Signor Achmet himself! If he favored the boy, there was no telling what riches might come to him. Perhaps the Signor wanted to buy a camel for the Sultan to ride. Perhaps he would be made second in command to the Signor and have a hundred slave-boys to come at the mere clapping of his hands.

His smile became a frightened squawk when Agba crumpled in a little heap at his feet.

With a swish of his robes, the driver dismounted, unwound his turban, and began fanning the boy. A crowd of men and boys gathered. They were full of words.

"The fast of Ramadan has weakened him."

"We saw him running beyond his strength."

"He is the first slaveboy of the Sultan's groom."

But only the camel driver worked over the boy, rubbing his hands, fanning him furiously. He held a leather water vessel to the boy's lips. Agba's eyelids flickered. He tried to drink. The water tasted warm and leathery. He hid his head in his arm.

The Arab was beside himself with worry. He *must* please this small emissary from the royal stables. He took one of the many identical goatskin bags from the camel's load, untied a drinking vessel, and poured out some of the precious camel's milk he was taking to market to sell. Then he added a few drops of wild honey and gave the cup to the boy.

Agba took a sip. He held the milk in his mouth. It

was thick and rich. It was both bitter and sweet at the same time, but it was good! He raised his eyes to the Arab's and smiled.

The Arab was transported with joy. He turned to the crowd about him, waving his arms wildly, showing his toothless gums in a broad grin.

He made Agba drink the full cup. Then he gave him a whole goatskin sack of milk to take along and a little jug of the wild honey besides. There would be time enough later to find out what the boy wanted.

"Go back now," he urged, "before the sun climbs higher. Sleep. Your message can wait."

As Agba walked away, hugging his precious gifts, the driver smiled, rubbing his hands together.

CAMEL'S MILK AND HONEY

WHEN AGBA REACHED SHAM'S STALL, he was afraid to open the door and look inside. Afraid that the colt would be gone too, and the stall would have that lonely, empty look that stalls take on when their occupants are dead.

He slipped inside and closed the door behind him. Now he looked. The colt was there! He was lying on his side, breathing so lightly that for a moment the boy was not sure. Then he took a step closer and smiled at his fears. The colt was alive, but oh, how thin and weak he was! His sides were almost as flat as Signor Achmet's prayer rug.

Agba took the goatskin sack from inside his vest, where he had held it close against his body to keep the milk warm. He filled a cup with it, adding some of the wild honey.

A whimper came from the tiny form on the straw.

Agba knelt down beside him. He stirred the milk with his fingers, then slid them into the colt's mouth.

The colt began working his mouth curiously. He bit the boy's fingers with his baby teeth. Then he sucked at them. Softly at first, then fiercely, with all the strength he had.

Agba dipped his fingers again and again. He had never known such happiness before. He made little purling noises in his throat. He made all sorts of promises in his mind. "My name is Agba. *Ba* means father. I will be a father to you, Sham, and when you are grown, the multitudes will bow before you. And you will be King of the Wind. I promise it."

The boy stirred the milk absently, lost in the future. It took the hungry bleating of the colt to bring him back. Sham was not concerned with having Agba for a father. What he wanted now was a mother. He nudged the horseboy with his pink muzzle. "More milk!" he whinnied.

The corners of Agba's mouth twisted into a smile. He went on with his feeding until Sham fell asleep.

Notwithstanding his dark prophecy, Signor Achmet seemed not in the least surprised when, day by day, Sham grew steadier on his finely drawn legs. "He will live," he said, in the same dry, cracked tone he had used when the mare died. "It is the will of Allah." Then he took to watching Agba through narrowed eyes, to see that he did not neglect the other horses.

Sham thrived on camel's milk and wild honey. And Agba thrived on Sham's worship to the point that there was a kind of hunger within him when the colt was out of his sight. And when the other boys so much as touched Sham's coat, his face clouded.

He moved Sham out of the brood-mare stable and into the stall of his dam. He brought his own hammock down from the horseboys' quarters and strung it in Sham's stall.

He made his prayers in Sham's stall, carefully

spreading his mantle to kneel on, and facing the eastern sky that showed itself through the round window at the back of the stall. After touching his head to the mantle, he formed the words with his lips, *"Allahouakibar!* God most great!" Then he rose, stretched his arms upward, his palms to the heavens, and made his own private prayer for Sham's welfare.

When the winds blew sharp and the rains came, he made a kind of flockbed mattress from wool fibers that he begged from a weaver. Part of it he slept on, and part he used to cover Sham and himself. Lying so, each took warmth and comfort from the other.

As Sham grew, he was turned out on grass with the spring colts. But by some quirk of nature they refused to accept him. Either they chewed at his brush of a tail and kicked up their heels at him, or they would have nothing at all to do with him. It was as if they thought he was too little to bother about.

Sham, however, seemed not to mind. He turned tail and larked across the paddock all by himself. He was busy learning about the world. He found that if he swiveled his ears, he could bring in sounds from behind — hoofbeats catching up to him; the pantherlike tread of Signor Achmet; the quick, pattering footfalls of Agba; the melody made by his own hoofs.

The world was full of wonders! If he stretched his nostrils to the wind, he could sift the most interesting smells — the delicious fragrance of clover; the biting smell of smoke from the burning stubble of cornfields; the perfume from orange and lime groves; the spicy aroma of pine woods beyond the city wall; the musky smell of the wild boar; the cool, moisture-laden scent of the clouds that blew over the snow-topped mountains. He could not label the smells as yet, but he was sorting them out in his mind.

Most important of all, he was toughening his muscles and sinews. He taught himself to wheel and plunge, and to run until he felt a soaring motion.

To Agba the world was full of wonders, too. One day when a flock of storks was migrating to Sudan, Agba watched in awe as he saw Sham skimming the earth trying to match their flight. Such a wonderment and pride filled him that it was almost as if he had foaled the little colt himself. He had never known such joy as these days brought! Here was a fellow creature that needed him. Not for food and water alone, but for comfort. When Sham was afraid, he came running to Agba for protection. When he was cold, he sidled up to Agba for warmth. When he was lonely, he nuzzled Agba and laid his satin nose against the boy's cheek.

What did it matter if the other colts thought Sham was different? He was! *They* ran to their mothers when they were hungry or in trouble. But Sham's mother was a slim brown horseboy.

THE SULTAN'S COMMAND

A YEAR PASSED. And another. And Sham fulfilled the promise of the white spot. He grew strong, and his fleetness surpassed that of his dam. Whenever the horseboys raced their horses beyond the city gates, Sham outran them all. He outran the colts his own age and the seasoned running horses as well. He seemed not to know that he was an

44

earthy creature with four legs, like other horses. He acted as if he were an airy thing, traveling on the wings of the wind. There came a time when none of the boys would challenge Agba's horse any more, for constant defeat took the heart out of their mounts.

One spring morning when Agba was watering the other horses in his charge, Signor Achmet tapped him on the shoulder. The Signor's face was drawn, and beads of perspiration dotted his upper lip.

"Agba," he said in a voice drained of all swagger, "Sultan Mulai Ismael commands me to appear before him this day, at the hour when the sun is in the center of the world. He commands six horseboys to accompany me."

The Signor's words quickened. "You, Agba, will be one of the six. When you have watered the horses, you will have your head shaved. The barber already awaits you. Then do you cleanse your body thrice over, from head to toe. Make ready."

Agba's eyes widened in terror. Sultan Mulai Ismael had reigned for over fifty years, and it was common knowledge that during his reign no horseboy summoned to the royal presence had ever returned. The Sultan was a fierce and bloodthirsty ruler. He thought nothing of ordering a thousand heads cut off to test the edge of a new saber. He thought nothing of commanding his soldiers to wipe out a whole village to test the power of his muskets.

Although the morning was warm, a chill of fear shook Agba from head to foot. If he did not return, who would there be to take care of Sham? Yet there was nothing to do but obey. He led the horses back to their stalls and went to the barber's courtyard behind the stables. The barber was already at work. Four of the boys were shaved clean, except for a small tuft of hair left growing from the very top of their heads. Agba's eyes noted the bloody scratches on the shaven places. Once he had watched a shepherd shear some mountain goats. He seemed far gentler than the barber.

Suddenly it was Agba's turn. The barber was sharpening his razor on a stone. Now he was skimming it over Agba's head. It felt as if each hair were being pulled up by its root. The only comforting thought was the barber's quickness. The ordeal would soon be over. Agba saw the other boys go to the well to draw water for their baths, and soon he was joining them.

Razor still in hand, the barber watched to see that the boys washed each finger and toe separately, and to make certain that they poured three vessels of water over themselves, each time washing their fingers and toes singly.

The sun was almost overhead when at last they stood ready, alike as six blades of grass. Red felt caps on each head. Long, coarse mantles with hoods. Bare, browned feet. And clutched in each bosom a chameleon for good luck.

In single file they joined Signor Achmet and marched down the long corridor between the stalls.

Plop, plop. Plop, plop. The soles of their feet made dull, thudding sounds on the earth. To Agba

they echoed the noise of his heart. *Plop, plop. Plop, plop.* Brown legs moved forward, alongside a high outer wall, then up and up a steep ramp to the entrance of the Sultan's sacred precincts.

Two rows of royal guards flanked the entrance. They stood so still they might have been a banding of sculptured figures. But Agba could feel their eyes upon him, stinging his flesh like sand particles driven by the wind. As the frightened company halted, six guards came to life. They opened wide the gate, made a sweeping bow to Signor Achmet, and waved him and his retinue inside.

It was a gallery they had entered, with gleaming white columns and arches fitted with glazed tiles bluer than the skies. *Plop, plop. Plop, plop.* The bare feet of the horseboys marched on, down the endless passageway where birds flew wildly as if seeking escape. On and on they went, through a second gate, through an inner court, through yet another gate. Agba shuddered as each gate closed behind him. It was like the sharp, crackling sound that comes with lightning. But no rumble of thunder followed. Only a stillness. It weighed on Agba's head, on his shoulders. It made breathing difficult.

Now, at a gate that was grander than the others,

a fierce-looking guard barred their progress. He pointed in disdain at Signor Achmet's head and his feet. Quickly the Signor threw back his hood and removed his slippers. The slaveboys had no slippers to take off, but they too dropped their hoods.

So, silently, the frightened company filed down the last gallery and came out upon the garden of Sultan Mulai Ismael, Emperor of all Morocco.

SIX STEEDS FOR A KING

WILD AND DISCORDANT MUSIC met their ears. Bagpipes, lutes, and tom-toms fought for supremacy. Agba did not heed them. Nor did he notice when the music stopped altogether, and gave way to the tinkling notes made by fountains of water playing in marble basins.

All his senses were trained on a wide dais at the end of the garden. There, sitting cross-legged on an embroidered red carpet, was Sultan Mulai Ismael himself.

The Sultan held the boy transfixed. He wore a towering white turban and a dazzling white robe with a golden sash. But what struck Agba was that in spite of the fine mantle and a beard whiter than driven snow, the old man reminded him of a camel. His eyes were hidden by heavy folds of eyelids, like a camel's, and his lips were thick and slit in two, and there was a big hump on his back. Even his feet were like those of a camel, spongy and broad and shapeless.

"Perhaps I am not going to be beheaded after all!" Agba thought. "The Sultan does not look like a man to be feared. He is nothing but a camel!"

Agba would not have been surprised in the least to see him rise up and swing along through the garden, stopping to feed on the leaves of the orange trees and the jasmine bushes.

Signor Achmet was kissing the Sultan's shoulder now, and bowing to the ground. Meanwhile a master of ceremonies placed each horseboy on one of the square tiles, like men on a chessboard. He arranged them behind the Signor, yet so placed that the Sultan could look full into the face of each boy.

Agba's eyes swept the throne. Squatting on small mattresses to the right of the Sultan sat the royal fly-flicker, the sword carrier, the slipper man, the teamaker. To the left were officers, messengers, and watchkeepers.

"Signor Achmet!" The Sultan broke the silence.

Frightened as he was, Agba wanted to laugh out, for even the Sultan's voice was high and shrill, like a camel that objects to being mounted.

"Signor Achmet!" he screaked. "I charge you, as head groom in the service of the Sultan of Morocco, to select six of the most perfect steeds in the royal stables. They will be a gift to His Majesty, Louis XV, the boy King of France."

The Sultan paused to let his words sink in. A fly buzzed close to his nose, and the fly-flicker deftly waved it away with a silken handkerchief.

"With six of your best horseboys," he went on, "you will accompany these steeds on their journey to the court of Versailles. And you will present them to the King in person."

So soft a sigh escaped the horseboys that it was lost in the little wind that stroked the trees.

"Seven days from this day," the Sultan was saying, "you will depart. At the exact moment, on the seventh day, when the sun strikes upon the tower of the mosque, you will come to the palace gate. It will be the hour of your going."

The Sultan twitched his thick lips. "A galleon already awaits you at Tangier. I have had stalls builded into its hold, complete with mangers. I have ordered a store of corn and chopped barley to be laid in on the day of your arrival in Tangier. Am I, or am I not, great?"

Signor Achmet bowed low. The personal attendants, the officers and messengers, the six horseboys, bowed low.

Mulai Ismael rocked back on his haunches. He wriggled his great shapeless toes. It was plain to see that he was enamored of this idea that had come to him. For a long moment he sat thus. Then he leaned forward abruptly. "Do you, or do you not, have a question?"

"Sire," asked the Signor, "shall the horses be mares or stallions?"

Agba listened so intently for the Sultan's answer that he wished the honeybees and flies would go about their business more quietly.

"Stallions!" the Sultan commanded, "to sire many sons of the desert.

"And no two," he added, as he curled his lips into a split smile, "shall be the same color. One shall be chestnut, deep-toned. And one shall be yellow dun, with tail and mane of silver. And one shall be dark gray, like the gray of the wood dove. And one shall be the whiteness of the flag that flies over the mosque at the hour of prayer. And one shall be black as a starless night. And one . . ."

The blood pounded in Agba's ears. Did not Mulai Ismael know that a bay horse was, of all horses, the most spirited?

The Sultan closed the thick folds of his eyelids. He leaned back, resting the weight of his turban against the blue tiles of the wall behind him. A hush came over the garden.

The fly-flicker leaped to his feet just in time to swerve a fly that was headed for the Sultan's uncovered feet.

"And one," the Sultan spoke at last, his voice high and far away, "and one shall be the color favored by the Prophet."

Agba's heart was hammering now. He thought of the white spot on Sham's heel. Only Sham was fit for a king. Only Sham . . .

Now the Sultan sat bolt upright. The folds of his eyes rolled back. "The sixth horse shall be a bay — not a dark bay, but a clear bay — whose coat is touched with gold. When he flees under the sun, he is the wind."

This time Agba's sigh was so deep that the sword-carrier and all the watch-keepers turned to look at him.

The Sultan, too, looked sharply, then went on. "Color," he said, "is but one qualification. Only the most perfect horses in the kingdom shall be chosen. Signor Achmet, you will measure each horse in the royal stables for proportion. You will begin at the withers and count the number of palms to the tail. Then do you measure from the withers along the neck up over the poll and down the face to the upper lip. If the distance of the fore part is greater than the hind part, the horse will travel like the wind, climb like the cat, and strike afar."

Agba's mind took wings. He and Sham were already in France. But the boy King was not mounting Sham. He was mounting the yellow dun, because no one but Agba could mount Sham. And together, Agba on Sham and the King on the yellow dun were riding tandem, cantering through the green forests.

Agba's daydreams ended in a start. The Sultan was clapping his spongy hands together. They sounded like hoofs in the mud. At once a white-robed scribe came hurrying out from behind the wall at the back of the throne. He was a shriveled, thin-faced creature, and in his arm he carried an ink horn, a quill pen, a sheaf of paper, and a white satin purse.

The Sultan waved him to a small mattress on his left. Quickly the scribe settled himself, dipped his pen in the ink, and with its point poised in mid-air waited for the Sultan's words.

"To the Most Noble, the Most Majestic King, Louis XV," the Sultan began. "That you may enjoy the years of Methuselah is the wish of my heart."

The scratching sound of the pen sent chills up and down Agba's spine. He had never before watched a man write.

Mulai Ismael mouthed each word slowly, as if it gave off a pleasant taste. "The bearer of this letter," he went on, "is chief groom in the service of His Majesty, Mulai Ismael, Sultan of Morocco. He is come with six Arabian stallions as a gift to Your Majesty. These Sons of the Desert are strong and fleet, and of purest Eastern blood. They are descended from mares that once belonged to Mohammed. From henceforward they are yours, that you may use them to sire a better race of horses among you. They will strengthen and improve your breed."

The Sultan narrowed his eyes at the half circle of horseboys. "Six horseboys," he said, letting each word fall sharply, "will accompany the six stallions. And each boy will care for the horse in his charge as long as that horse shall live. Upon the death of the horse, the boy shall return at once to Morocco."

Agba did not hear the rest of the letter at all. Drums were beating inside him. "*As long as that horse shall live. As long as that horse shall live.*"

The secretary finished the letter and read it aloud.

"It wants a word," the Sultan said. "Insert 'my' before 'respects.' I charge you then to stamp it with the seal of Mulai Ismael."

With great exactness, the scribe inserted the word "my" in its proper place. Then he opened his white satin purse and spilled the contents — a piece of red wax, a seal, and a silken cord — on the mattress. A slaveboy appeared from nowhere, almost as if he had come out of the purse too. He held a candle for the scribe to melt the wax. Agba watched as the man dropped a stain of red on the paper and stamped it with the seal. Then he held the seal to his forehead, kissed it, rolled the letter into a scroll, and tied it with the silken cord.

Old Mulai Ismael beamed with satisfaction. A present of six Arabian stallions would make Monsieur le Duc, the King's adviser, rub his hands with pleasure. Each horse could win big stakes on the racecourse for him.

The Sultan's little eyes gleamed in anticipation of all the favors he would receive in return: the hogsheads of claret, the coffee and tea and brocades, a royal carriage no doubt! But most important, Monsieur le Duc would close his eyes to the Sultan's bloody rule.

The Sultan felt good. He nodded to the teamaker, and with that nod the garden burst into activity. Slaveboys came running from every direction. Some began washing the Sultan's hands, sprinkling his turban, his beard, his shoulders, his feet, with perfumed water. Others came bearing a low, round eating table covered over with a hood made of palm leaves.

The teamaker lifted the hood and there, glittering in the spring sunshine, was a gold teapot, sending forth a little jet of steam. He dropped a packet of tea into the pot and added ginger and cloves and mint and thyme, and as many loaves of sugar as he could hold in the cup of his hand. Then he stepped over to the sundial and watched the time pass.

The fragrance of steaming tea and spices filled the garden. The narrow slits of the Sultan's nose widened. The horseboys sniffed audibly.

At a nod from the teamaker, a guard sampled the tea. He took a second swallow, then wiped his beard on his mantle. The tea had not been poisoned.

Mulai Ismael reached for a cup. "Give it me!" he demanded. He drank three cupfuls in quick succession, then sipped a fourth with great deliberation. At last he ordered that everyone in the garden be served.

Agba looked at the beautiful amber color of the tea. He took a sip. He savored it slowly. It was good.

Over the gold rim of his cup, the Sultan's eyes wandered over the horseboys and stopped at Agba.

"Come near unto me," he commanded.

Agba's teacup dropped to the tile and shattered.

"Come near unto me!" repeated the Sultan, his shrill voice climbing to the breaking point.

Slowly, clutching his chameleon to his breast,

the boy walked past Signor Achmet, past the squatting scribe and the officers and guards, until he stood so close to the Sultan that he could smell the oriental perfume with which his garments were scented. The cloying sweetness made him feel sick.

"The King of France is just about the age of this boy; perhaps a trifle older," the Sultan remarked. He fixed the boy with his eyes. "How old are you?" he asked of Agba.

A heavy silence was the answer.

"Speak up! How old are you?" he repeated, his voice rasping in anger.

Again a heavy silence.

The Sultan's hand fingered the stiletto that hung from his belt. It tightened until the leathery knuckles whitened.

A cold perspiration came out all over Agba's body. He opened his mouth, but no sound came. No sound whatever.

Suddenly a soft rustling noise behind him broke the terrible silence. It was made by the garments of Signor Achmet.

"Your Majesty," he began, hesitatingly. "May I speak?"

"Speak out quickly," the Sultan said, drawing his stiletto.

Signor Achmet's voice was hushed. "The horse-boy, Agba, has no power of speech."

"What!"

"Aye, sire."

Now even the horseboys gasped. They did not know that Agba was a mute. They remembered, now that they thought about it, that Agba talked with his fiery black eyes, his thin hands, his shoulders, his eyebrows, and with his silences.

The Signor nodded his head. "The boy is a mute."

"Can he manage a horse?"

"Aye, Your Majesty."

"Then I charge you to take him with you to the court of Versailles. A boy who cannot talk can spill no tales." With a gesture of impatience he returned his stiletto to its sheath. Then he peered at the position of the sun and nodded a curt dismissal to Signor Achmet.

Agba stood still. He felt he had no strength to move. But the audience was ended. Signor Achmet struck him lightly on the shoulder. With the groom and the horseboys he bowed low before the Sultan and walked backward out of the garden.

As soon as they reached the outer gate, Agba freed the chameleon in his bosom. Then he listened for the footfalls of his little company. No longer did they go *plop, plop, plop, plop*. They were so light and springy they made no sound at all.

The other horseboys broke into excited chatter as they started toward the stables. But Agba was thinking only of Sham.

AGBA MEASURES SHAM

I T WAS ALMOST SUNDOWN before Agba had a moment to measure Sham. With fast-beating heart
he ran his hand along the horse's back until he
came to the tail. Then he stopped. One! he counted
in his mind. He placed his left hand ahead alongside his right. Two! He crossed his right hand

over his left. Three! He brought his left hand around to his right. Four! Each time he spread out his fingers to make his hand as broad as Signor Achmet's.

The count at the withers was fifteen. He leaned his head against Sham's neck, afraid to go on.

What if the count from withers to muzzle would be less than fifteen hands, or only equal to fifteen? A thousand horrible thoughts flew into his mind. Sham left behind, Sham mistreated by another horseboy, a whip lashed across his body, spurs kicked into his ribs, the sand in his stall unchanged.

Sham nudged Agba's shoulder, scratching his nose on the boy's coarse mantle. Agba straightened. He could put off the moment no longer. Signor Achmet would soon be here. "I will get to your corridor at sundown," he had told Agba. "In all the royal stables there are but four bay stallions touched with gold. Already I have measured three. One qualifies. His hind part measures fifteen hands, his fore part eighteen."

Agba resumed his measuring. Fingers trembling, he placed his right hand on Sham's withers. One! Left hand came alongside. Two! Right over left. Three! Left alongside right. Four!

Right, left. Five, six.

Twelve at the crest.

Fifteen at the ears.

Now over the poll and down the face. Right, left. Sixteen. Seventeen.

Right, left. Eighteen. Nineteen.

Nineteen at the upper lip!

At that moment Agba felt the knotted stick on his shoulder. He wheeled around and faced the Signor.

The Signor's head was nodding up and down. "Aye," he was saying. "This one is chosen. He measures one hand more than the best. His neck is made long to stretch out in running."

The Signor turned and was gone. Agba quickly closed the door of the stall behind him. Wild with excitement, he kissed the white spot on Sham's heel. He sprang up on Sham's back, and with his hands for a neck rein, he rode him around and around the stall until they both were dizzy.

The seven days before their departure flew. Agba made a nosebag out of his turban to accustom Sham to the way he would have to eat on the overland journey to Tangier. He exercised him, increasing the distance each day. He took him to the farrier's and watched, troubled, as the big-muscled man took a knife and a hammer and fitted Sham's hooves to the shoes. Both he and Sham were covered with sweat when the shoeing was finally done.

On the last night in the Sultan's stables, Agba hardly slept at all. He kept jumping down from his hammock and feeling inside the two great pockets which fitted over the cantle of his saddle. He wanted to make sure that nothing was missing: the leathern vessel for water, the fine new nosebag the Signor had given him; the rub-rag made of camel's hair; the little earthen jug of rancid butter, called *budra,* with which to rub Sham's legs; the fly crop made from the hairs of Sham's tail.

The stars were beginning to fade when at last he slept.

SALEM ALICK!

BY THE TIME DAWN CREPT DOWN the Atlas
Mountains and filled the Meknes valley with
long shafts of light, Signor Achmet and six horseboys, on their Arabian stallions, were on their
way to the royal palace.

Agba, first of the six, rode with his eyes fixed on

the sun. It was climbing higher and higher, veering southward, nearer and nearer to the tower of the mosque. Now its outer rim was almost touching the slender needle.

The Signor, too, was watching the sun. If he did not arrive at the exact moment the Sultan had specified, there was no telling what the punishment might be. He quickened his pace. Agba and the other boys did not need to urge their horses. They were eager to go, tossing their heads with impatience. Just as the sun slid behind the tower, the procession moved up the steep incline that led to the entrance of the palace grounds.

And at that precise moment four bagpipers and four tom-tom players tore the morning stillness to shreds. The palace gates were flung open, and Sultan Mulai Ismael himself came riding toward them. He swayed on his horse like a ship at sea, and in his wake trailed an enormous following — the parasol holder, the fly-flickers, the groom, the spurmen, and slaves and foot soldiers without number.

There was a flurry of movement along the walls. A thousand guards stood at attention. A thousand spears, like so many serpents' tongues, were thrust into the air. A thousand throats shouted above the drums and the bagpipes, "May Allah bless the life of our Sultan!"

Signor Achmet and the horseboys bowed until their noses brushed the manes of their mounts. Without answering the salutation, the royal procession swept past them, down the incline between rows of guards, and led the way to the city gates.

In single file the Signor and the horseboys followed. Through the narrow public streets they rode. Buyers and sellers and saints and beggars joined the parade.

Women, their faces half-hidden by veils, came out on the rooftops to watch and to add their high-voiced cries to the beating of the tom-toms and the skirling of the bagpipes.

Discordant as the music was, there was a kind of rhythm and excitement to it, too. The horses kept time to it. The silken handkerchiefs of the fly-flickers, and even the royal parasol, waved to its rhythm.

As the parade left the market place, Agba felt someone pull at his mantle. He looked out of the corner of his eye and caught the toothless grin of the camel driver.

Agba smiled in quick recognition.

The camel driver bellowed a huzza. Then he extended his arms to heaven, as if this moment of

sharing Agba's glory was reward enough for all the camel's milk he had given him.

At last the procession reached the outer gate of the city. The music stopped. A great silence fell over the multitude as the Sultan, helped by his attendants, dismounted. With a jolting, camel-like trot he made his way to the six Arabians and tied a silken bag around the neck of each one. There was a dark red bag for the chestnut, a pale yellow one for the yellow dun, a gray bag for the dappled gray, a white bag for the white, a black one for the black, and for Sham there was a bag made of shiny gold cloth.

The Sultan's shrill voice pierced the quiet.

"These bags," he said, "contain the pedigree of each stallion. They also contain amulets of great power, amulets that will prevent and cure the bite of scorpions and protect your stallions from evil spirits. Guard these bags well. The King of France and Monsieur le Duc will thus bear witness to my greatness." He patted his chest and grinned until his eyes were hidden in their folds of fat.

"Ride under the sun," his voice intoned. "Ride under the rain water, blessed of Allah. Ride the golden hills of the Atlas Mountains. Ride through the green valleys and the regions of the plains.

71

Ferry across the winding rivers. And when you have crossed the provinces of Errif and El Garb, then do you embark at Tangier and sail the blue waters of the Mediterranean. Travel in safety, so that the King and Monsieur le Duc will thus bear witness to my greatness."

He turned to Signor Achmet. His voice changed. "Give your horses the heel!" he shrieked. "*Salem alick!* Farewell!"

"*Alick salem!*" cried the Signor. Then, clapping his spurs to his horse, he wheeled and rode out of the gate, followed by the six purest-bred stallions in the kingdom of Morocco.

In the twinkling of an eye, horses and riders were gone, speeding toward the ship prepared for them.

The Sultan returned to his palace with a smile of satisfaction, thinking how neatly his plans were working out.

He did not know that the captain of the vessel had pocketed the money sent to buy corn and barley for the horses and had stuffed the sacks with straw instead. Nor did he know that the horseboys would be made to man the heavy sails on stormy seas. Nor that day after day they would be fed only on bread and water, until they were skin and bones when at last they reached the coast of France.

THE BOY KING

IT WAS FOUR WEEKS LATER to a day when Signor Achmet and his little company arrived at the court of Versailles. Monsieur le Duc, the King's adviser, was in the beauty salon at the time. He was calmly admiring himself in a mirror, when suddenly the pixie-like face of the King's groom was reflected right alongside his own.

"My Lord Duke! My Lord Duke!" the groom puffed. "I have news! News!"

"What brings you to the beauty salon?" Monsieur spoke in an icy tone. "Is the stable afire?"

"Oh no, my Lord."

"What is it then?" he asked, viewing the back of his wig with a long-handled mirror.

The elfin figure of the groom was agitated with excitement. "Why, 'tis a gift to His Majesty, the King," he breathed. "A gift of six horses. They stand within the stable this very moment."

"Ha!" scoffed Monsieur le Duc. "A hundred horses are in the royal stables. Yet you disturb my toilet with news of a paltry six more."

"But, my Lord! They've come by land and by sea all the way from . . ."

"Hold your tongue!" the Duke commanded. He turned to the gentleman-of-the-wigs. "You shall add forty more curls," he said, rolling the words on his tongue as if he were tasting a French pastry. "You shall do twenty on either side, to form the effect of pigeons' wings. What think you of it?"

The gentleman-of-the-wigs raised the fingers of his right hand as if he were holding a teacup.

"*Exactement!*" he grimaced. "Forty it shall be!

Twenty on either side! It will be my masterpiece!" And he whisked the wig from Monsieur's head, carefully replacing it with the old wig which, to the eyes of the groom, looked almost identical.

The Duke turned to the groom. "Whence did you say the horses came?" he snapped.

"I did not say, my Lord."

"Well, speak up!"

"From Africa, my Lord. From Morocco. And, my Lord, the bearer of the gift and his six horse-boys will not leave the stable."

"What's that? What's that?"

"They stand like stones. They will *not* leave. The chief fellow has a letter, and he will give it to no one but Monsieur le Duc or His Majesty the King." The groom tiptoed around the gentleman-of-the-wigs and brought his face close to the Duke's. "Methought you'd like to know," he whispered, "that I have the King's horse in readiness. In a moment he leaves for the chase. But, my Lord," the groom's face broke into a sly smile, "methought *you* would like to come to the stable and read the letter first."

Monsieur le Duc patted the groom's shoulder with a jeweled hand. Then, upsetting a powder table in his haste, he snatched up his plumed hat and hurried to the stables with the groom running bowlegged behind him.

As Mulai Ismael's letter was being put into the Duke's hands, King Louis XV, followed by twenty courtiers, walked into the royal stable. A great stillness seemed to come in with them. The only sound in that vast high-ceilinged building was made by Sham swishing a fly from his hip.

The young King stopped stock still. He seemed transfixed by the pitiful gathering before him. Slowly, looking from one to the other, he studied the six stallions and the lead horse of Signor Achmet. They were carefully groomed, but so bony that each rib showed. And beside each stallion stood a thin, ragged horseboy, holding his charge on a lead rope.

The King was about the same age as the horseboys, but there the likeness stopped. He wore high polished boots and golden spurs, and his breeches and coat were of velvet. The horseboys were barelegged, and the insides of their legs were covered with blue-green welts made by their stirrup straps on the long overland ride. And their bodies were wrapped in coarse, hooded cloaks.

Agba was glad of the hood. It was like the pro-

tective shell of a turtle. He could see out, yet he felt that no one could see him. Had he only known, the darkness of his hood made glowing embers of his eyes.

Monsieur le Duc cleared his throat. He bowed low. "Your Majesty," he sniveled, "may find this letter interesting. I know not what it says."

Louis XV looked past the Duke as if he did not exist.

"Read it to me," he said absently, without taking his eyes from the horses or the boys.

"It bears the seal of Mulai Ismael," the Duke said as he untied the silken cord and broke the red seal. His tongue passed rapidly over the complimentary phrases at the beginning. Then he read more slowly.

" 'The bearer of this letter is come with six Arabian stallions as a gift to Your Majesty. These sons of the desert are strong and fleet . . .' "

Here the Duke burst out laughing. "Really, Your Majesty, this is very amusing. The Sultan refers to these bags of bones as 'strong and fleet and of purest Eastern blood.' Pardon me, Your Majesty, but it is enough to make me die of laughter."

At the sound of his hollow laughter all the horses laced their ears back.

78

The King's face clouded. "Read on," he said.

"Very well. 'They are descended from mares that once belonged to Mohammed.'" Now the Duke's voice was full of mockery and scorn. "'From henceforward,' the letter reads, 'you may use them to sire a better race of horses among you. They will strengthen and improve your breed.'"

The King's groom brought forward his mount. The horse was a big gelding, nearly twice the size of the Arabians. From his superior height, he looked down on the six stallions and let out a shrill whinny.

The Duke shrieked with laughter. "See there, Your Majesty! Even your own horse is laughing. I trust you will send these old sand sifters back to the desert where they belong. The bony broomtails!"

Agba's fists clenched. He could not understand a word of this foreign tongue, but he knew that the man was laughing at Sham and the other horses. His burning eyes sought the King's. He longed to tell him that the horses were gaunt only because of the terrible journey, and that soon they would be sleek and beautiful again. He longed to tell him how swift they were, and how brave.

"Send a messenger to Bishop Fleury," the King

said to the groom. "Tell him the King awaits him."

The courtiers who were clustered behind the King drew a sigh. This was all very much like a play. Act One was over. Now there would be a little wait for Act Two.

Monsieur le Duc made his own use of the intermission. He drew a tiny snuff bottle out of his pocket and dipped into it with a miniature silver spoon. Then he fed each nostril a rounded spoonful of the snuff.

"Your Majesty," he said, pinching his nose and snuffing noisily. "Mulai Ismael insults the horses of France. He insults your own mount. But more dastardly, he insults your Royal Majesty."

Making a wry face, he let his glance wander over the chestnut, the dappled gray, the yellow dun, the black horse, the moon-colored horse. When he came to Sham, he stopped short. "Monstrosity!" he spat out the word. "Nothing but skin and bones, and a crest so high you can hang your hat upon it! Fie! Pooh! Bah!"

His face wrinkled until it looked not much bigger than a prune. Then the prune seemed to burst open, and the very stable trembled with the force of the Duke's sneeze.

Sham wheeled in fright. And to Agba's horror

his off hind hoof landed squarely on Monsieur le Duc's toe.

Quick as a flash, Agba lifted Sham's foot. He could not help noticing, with the faintest of smiles, that it was the one with the white spot.

With a mighty outcry, the Duke grabbed his foot and went hopping about the stable like a one-legged bird.

"Help! Help ho!" he cried while the courtiers and the horseboys tittered. Agba thought he saw a smile flicker across the King's face, but he could not be sure. Bishop Fleury had arrived.

Agba liked the Bishop at once. He had friendly blue eyes and wore no wig at all. His hair was powdered white by time. He bowed to the King first, then turned to the Duke, his eyes crinkled with suppressed laughter. "What is it, Monsieur le Duc? What is it?" he asked.

Monsieur le Duc's face was stained an angry red.

"This — this clumsy, camel-necked nag!" he stammered. "He crushed my toe. What is more, he did it from a vile temper and . . ."

"The Sultan's letter," the King interrupted. "I desire you to show it to Bishop Fleury."

"Read it to me, Monsieur le Duc," said the Bishop. "My eyes are fading."

Monsieur le Duc spared nothing in the reading. At the end he said, "I beg your pardon, Bishop Fleury, but the rains have spoiled the harvest. Corn is scarce. My advice to the King is to send these nags of small stature back to Africa." His eyes fell on Sham. "Save one," he added. "The chief cook is in need of a cart horse to drive to market."

The King looked to the Bishop with questioning eyes.

"Dear son," the Bishop said as he put a gentle hand on the boy's head. "Pray look at your own stableful of horses. Pray look at your favorite mount. He is stout of limb, and lusty. These Arabian creatures are small. Moreover, corn is dear. Why do you not turn the high-crested creature over to the chief of the kitchen? He could draw a cart to market and bring back the food for your table. The other horses could be assigned to the army to transport supplies. They would thus need far less to eat than if they were employed in the chase."

Agba's and the King's eyes met. It was the King who looked down first. He was King in name only. He had no power to change the order of the older men. He nodded his head listlessly. "Let it be as you say." And without another glance at the stallions he mounted his great horse and rode away.

THE THIEVES' KITCHEN

O NLY AGBA AND SHAM REMAINED in the King's stables. Signor Achmet dared not go back to Morocco and face the wrath of the Sultan. He swallowed his pride and went along with the other horseboys, accepting a humble position as groom in the French army. Before he left, however, he took the bag from Sham's neck and tied it around

83

Agba's. "The pedigree and the amulets will be safer with you, Agba," he said, with a meaningful look at the King's groom.

In the days that followed, Sham regained his vigor. And with it seemed to come an intense distrust of everyone except Agba. With Agba in the driver's seat, Sham's way of going to market was so bold and handsome that journeymen turned round to gape at him. He pranced his way between the stalls of the pea shellers and the artichoke boilers as if he were making figure eights in the King's courtyard. As for the harness and the degrading vehicle he pulled, one would have thought he wore purple housings and drew the King's carriage!

But if the chief cook so much as touched the reins, Sham took the bit and went where he pleased, and no amount of whiplashing could control him. The people in the market place stood in open-mouthed wonder at the spirit of Sham. Secretly they admired the proud way he took the cook's lashes. There was the plump apple woman who polished her apples with her apron. She soon made it a habit each market day to save two of her biggest apples — one for the fiery little horse and the other for the quiet boy. Even the vendor of sweets held back a pan of frosted pastries on the days when Sham was expected. And a farmer who had the turnip stall managed to keep from his wife a whole sackful of turnips for Sham.

One day the chief cook insisted upon driving alone to market. He wanted to select a nice suckling pig for the King's birthday dinner. "And," he told Agba, "I need every inch of space for the live pig and for sausages and potatoes and mushrooms and herrings and eggs and chickens. You will stay in the kitchen and scour the pots."

Now the cook told Agba only half the truth. What he really wanted was to be rid of Agba. It irked him that a mere sliver of a boy could manage the horse and he could not. If he could just get rid of the boy, he had a feeling he could master the horse.

But he was wrong. Without Agba, Sham was mischief itself. He waited until the cart was groaning with vegetables and fish and fowl and the live pig. Then suddenly he became forked lightning. In and out among the market stalls he streaked. He overturned the cart, spewing chickens, herrings, eggs, the frightened pig, and an amazed cook high into the air!

Children screamed. Fishmongers, marketwomen,

eating-house keepers slipped and stumbled. They shook their fists and shouted at the King's cook.

As he scrambled to his feet, the cook was so confused he did not know whether to chase the horse or the suckling pig! He darted first after one and then the other, and ended by catching neither. When the little apple woman quietly held out her hand and brought Sham to a halt, it was more than the cook could bear. He was beside himself with rage.

"This settles it!" he cried. "Everyone but me can handle the crazy brute. I'll sell him at the Horse Fair."

To horse traders, the Horse Fair was known by quite a different name. It was called the Thieves' Kitchen, because no one knew where the horses came from and nobody cared. No questions were asked.

Red-faced and panting, the cook led Sham to the big open shed of the Thieves' Kitchen. Sham was not winded in the least. He seemed actually to be enjoying the cook's discomfiture.

The cook cast a quick glance to the right and to the left. In all the long shed there was not another horse trader in sight. He sighed with relief, for the fewer people who saw him in his disheveled condition the less talk there would be. If word of the lost pig and the runaway horse ever reached the royal kitchen, his high position would be ruined. The scullions, as they cleaned their pots and kettles, would whisper and laugh behind his back. He must sell the horse quickly. He resolved to get rid of him to the very first buyer.

Scarcely had he blotted the splattered eggs from his overblouse when a man walked past. He was enormous in build, and he stalked rather than walked, like a big tiger cat. His hat was pulled far down over his head, and he looked neither to the one side nor to the other. Yet somehow the cook sensed that the man was in the vicinity of Thieves' Kitchen for but one purpose. He was in need of a horse.

Almost past the shed, he wheeled about and came skulking back, shaking his head as if suddenly remembering an errand.

The cook could not see the face of the man, but he noticed the brutish size of him — hands big and broad, legs shaped like water casks. He noticed, too, that the man carried a horsewhip. A wood carter, he figured. Or a street hawker.

"Ahem!" the cook cleared his throat. "Are you in need of a stout beast, sir?"

The man stopped in his tracks.

"No!" he snarled, pulling his hat even farther over his eyes. "Your price is too high."

"But sir," wheedled the cook, "I have not spoken to you about the price."

"I know you thieves," the carter bawled out, waving the cook aside. "You steal a horse. Then ask a fortune for it."

A group of passers-by and idlers began surrounding the two men.

The cook spoke in a low tone. "Name *your* price, my good man, and I'll throw in the harness too, and a slightly damaged cart with a few vegetables in it. He's a good stout beast, he is."

"Why, that weed!" the carter threw back his head and bellowed. "He's neither horse nor pony. Too small for one, too big for the other. Besides, his neck's misshaped!"

"But sir," pleaded the cook, "you've not even looked at the creature."

The carter motioned the growing crowd to close in. He thumped himself on the chest with the handle of his whip. "Me and all my friends here," he roared, "we saw the whole show. Ho! Ho!" he snorted, "the beast made a fool out of you. He freed your pig and scrambled your eggs. Ho! Ho! Ho!"

Then he brushed the people aside and began fumbling in his pockets, taking a little money from each one. I'll give you these francs for the nag," he said. "Then I'll teach him a thing or two." And he cracked his whip sharply as if to prove his words.

Sham felt the gust of wind made by the whip. He quivered, then went up on his hind legs and neighed shrilly.

The cook laughed. He was not interested in Sham's feelings. He was interested only in getting rid of the horse. That the man was brutish concerned him not at all. Quickly the deal was closed, and the carter led Sham away.

AGBA BECOMES AN AWAKENER

WHEN THE CHIEF COOK RETURNED ALONE, his clothes torn and his face grim, Agba knew that Sham was in trouble. He was beside himself with worry. He dogged the man's footsteps, but he could learn only that Sham had been left in Paris. Why or where, the cook stubbornly refused to tell.

Finally he became so annoyed at Agba's shadow that he booted the boy out of the kitchen door. "You, you tagtail!" he bawled out after him. "Stay out of my sight. Go find the beast yourself."

Agba fled to Paris. He haunted the market place, the Horse Fair, the stables of the inns. Night and day he searched the roads that led into the great city. He lived on nothing but apples which the apple woman gave him. When he did sleep, he curled up in a nest of straw in the very shed where Sham had been sold.

One night the owner of a chocolate shop offered him a job as an awakener. "Ye seldom seem to sleep anyway," he told Agba. "Ye may as well be paid for waking others. Besides, ye look as if ye needed some steaming chocolate to warm your belly and a kind word to warm your heart."

Agba was glad of the work. The chocolate shop was in the center of the market district, and served carters and buyers. One among them might turn out to be the owner of Sham.

Each night now he snatched a few hours of sleep in the shed at the Horse Fair. Then, long before sunrise, he would hurry to the chocolate shop, drink his pot of chocolate, and go to work. It was his job, as soon as the market stalls were ready for business, to awaken the customers who had arrived in the middle of the night and had fallen asleep over their cups.

Some slept so deeply that no amount of shaking would rouse them. They had almost to be lifted to their feet. These heavy sleepers paid Agba two sous. The light sleepers paid him one sou. A few laughed in his face and did not pay him at all.

One early summer evening when Agba was on his way to the shed, he decided to wander along the Boulevard St. Denis and wait for dark to fall. He stopped to watch the play of water in a marble fountain. There was something about the tinkling sound that reached far back into his memory. The street faded away. In its place was the Sultan's garden. Agba could smell the orange blossoms and jasmine. He could hear the Sultan's voice: "And one shall be a clear bay touched with gold."

He was hardly aware of the sound of cartwheels and the *clomp-clomp* of unshod hooves. Yet he closed the shutter on his dreams and, from force of habit rather than hope, turned to look at the animal.

Something within him snapped. A small dusty horse, harnessed to an empty cart, was coming toward him. The horse turned toward the fountain

92

as if to drink, but the driver jerked him sharply away.

Agba's heart seemed to stop altogether, then suddenly began thumping. He waved to the man to stop.

"Aside! You dog!" roared the carter as he struck Agba's legs with the lash of his long whip.

Agba jumped aside, his eyes never leaving the horse. He tried to make the little purling noises in his throat, but they would not come. No matter. This beaten creature could not be Sham. It was only the size that brought up his memory. There was no wheat ear on his chest. Or . . . could it be hidden by the collar of his harness? There was no white spot on his off hind heel. Or . . . could it be crusted with mud?

Agba followed the cart past a big inn, past a theater of marionettes, past houses with gabled roofs that stared down at him with their triangular eyes, then down squalid old streets and narrow passages. *Clop, clop. Clop, clop. Clop, clop.* Once the horse stumbled, and Agba could hear the loud curses of the driver. Then *clop, clop. Clop, clop.* And just when Agba could bear the sound no longer, the horse turned into an extremely narrow alley and stopped before a rickety shed.

Hiding behind a barrel, Agba peered around and saw that half of the shed was empty, the other half piled to the rafters with wood. He watched as a cat leaped out from the woodpile, streaked toward the horse, and landed lightly on his back. A weak whinny escaped the horse, but it was lost in the carter's scorn. "Grimalkin! You crazy tomcat!" he taunted, "still in love with your bony friend?"

Agba saw the cart drawn into the shed, saw the driver hitch the horse to a ring on the wall, toss him a bundle of hay, and walk off into the deepening twilight.

Slowly, slowly, the boy stole into the shed. He walked around the cart until at last he was standing face to face with the horse. He was near enough to touch the muzzle, near enough to stroke the gaunt neck, but he forced his hands to hang at his sides. Now the cat was mewing softly, and to his voice the boy added the only sounds he could make, the little purling noises like a brook on a summer's day.

The ears of the horse began to twitch. His nostrils quivered. Then without a sound he lowered his head and rubbed it against Agba's shoulder.

Agba did not need to look for the wheat ear or the white spot. It was Sham!

A STRANGE THREESOME

THE CARTER ALLOWED AGBA to live in his shed, not from kindness but because he could use the boy. He had long wanted someone to load his cart each morning. Now a slave had come to him as if by magic. And it cost him nothing at all — in money or food or clothing.

Agba gave up his job as awakener. Instead, he helped the fishmongers and the farm women at the market place by day, and so came to the alley at night with presents of little things that horses and cats like.

It was a strange threesome: the boy, the cat, and the horse. Each evening, at the first sound of cart-wheels, Grimalkin would fly out of the shed. With a quick leap he was on Sham's back, miaowing and talking to him in his cat's way.

Agba would wait in silence, wait for the creaking wheels to come to a stop, wait for the deep bellowing roar of the carter. Always it was the same.

"You mute! You numps! A horse and a cat for company! Out of my way!"

At first the carter let Agba unharness Sham at night and tend his sores, but when he saw the fiery look return to Sham's eyes he was not pleased. And when, one day, Sham seized him by the breeches and bit him viciously, the carter flew into a rage.

"The brute can sleep harnessed and standing," he told Agba. "A few harness sores'll teach him to respect this!" And he snaked his whip in the air until it hissed.

On Sundays, however, the carter never came near

the shed, and it seemed as if all day long the cat never stopped purring and Sham neighed his happiness in a pitiful, thin sound. As for Agba, there was a silent rapture in the way he worked. He washed Sham. He dried and smoothed his coat. He rubbed the horse's legs with the last of the *budra* which he had brought from Africa. He combed Sham's tangled tail and mane. He made cooling poultices of wet leaves, and applied them with gentle fingers to all of Sham's sores. He packed the inner walls of Sham's hooves with mud. And he fed him three times a day with the oats he had bought with his own money.

As Agba ran his hand over the wheat ear on Sham's chest or the white spot on his heel, the words of Signor Achmet kept beating in his ears: "The white spot against the wheat ear. The good sign against the bad. The one and the other."

The days shortened into winter. Despite Agba's care, Sham's coat was not coming in thick and glossy as it had in Morocco. It remained harsh and staring. And some nights he was too tired to eat. He would only mouth the food that Agba brought, and drop it listlessly. Day by day Agba watched the skin of Sham's neck grow more and more flabby, and the hollow places above his eyes deepen.

One fierce, cold morning, in the dead of winter, the carter startled the three creatures out of their sleep with a shrill whistle. He stood over them, rubbing his hands in pleasure. *This* was the kind of day he liked. Last night's sleet had stopped. The air was sharpening. People would need plenty of wood to feed their fires. Business would be brisk.

He stood with hands on hips, singing a coarse song while Agba loaded the cart. Usually he was satisfied when the load reached the top of the great cartwheels. But this day he ordered the logs laid higher and higher, and he kicked Agba when the boy tried to interfere. At last he had to help tie the logs with a stout hempen cord to keep them from toppling.

"Ho! Ho!" he sang out lustily as he swung his great hulking body atop the load, "I feel sorry for beasts on a frosty day like this, so I give 'em a big load to make 'em sweat. *Allons!*" he shouted, cracking his whip.

Agba saw Sham slip on the icy ramp that led out of the shed. He saw the carter pull him up by a savage tug on the bit. Then horse and cart were lost in the darkness.

Shopkeepers were opening their shutters, and the tallow dips of the city were being snuffed out when the carter reached the Boulevard St. Denis.

His first stop was at the Hôtel de Ville, a big gray building with lions at the entrance. To get to the service entrance, Sham had to climb a steady upgrade from the street. But try as he would, he could get no footing on the icy cobble stones. Balls of ice had formed inside his hooves, and after many tries he was still pawing and slipping at the very bottom of the incline.

The carter's temper was growing short. He laid the whip across Sham's bony hips. He stood up and lashed it across the horse's ears. He shouted and cursed.

"You tom-noddy! You puny nag! Back up, you beast of a carthorse!"

Icicles were forming on Sham's feelers, yet his body was wet with sweat. He backed up. He lowered his head, and as the whip struck him, he made a snatching pull. The load moved, and as if by some supernatural power Sham kept on going up the incline. When almost at the top, however, his forefeet began slipping. He clawed with them. The whip snarled and cracked. It cut deep into his hide. Groaning, he tried again, and again. His veins swelled to bursting.

In spite of the bitter weather, passers-by stopped

to watch. A water carrier set down his yoke and stepped forward as if to protest. But one look at the livid face of the carter stopped him.

Sham was sucking for breath, his nostrils going in and out, showing the red lining. Once more he threw himself against the collar of his harness. He struggled to keep his footing. The onlookers were pulling with him, breathing heavily, tensing their muscles as one man, straining, straining to help. But it was no use. With a low moan, Sham fell to his knees.

A great crowd had gathered, and a collection of dogs began barking as the carter jerked the reins, trying to lift Sham up by sheer force. But he was caught fast between the shafts of the cart. His eyes were wild and white-ringed with fear, his mouth bleeding.

Leaping to the paving stones, the carter braced the cart with a log. "Now," he yelled to the crowd, "I'll take my own faggots and build a fire under his tail. That'll make the stubborn beast rise!"

As he was reaching for his faggots, an Englishman of stately bearing made his way into the crowd. He wore the collarless black coat and the broad-brimmed black hat of a Quaker. Although his garments and manner were sober, there was a fiery look in his eye.

"My friend," he addressed the carter in perfect French, "I have long wanted a quiet old horse." Opening his greatcoat he drew from his inner pocket a handful of gold. "I am prepared," he said coolly, "to offer fifteen louis for the creature."

At sight of the gold, the carter's mouth went agape. A greedy light leaped into his eyes. He dropped the faggots. "Fifteen louis for a done-up nag?" he asked incredulously.

"Aye, friend," the Quaker nodded. "I have need of a smallish horse for my son-in-law, Benjamin Biggle."

Even the onlookers were round-eyed now. Why, fifteen louis would buy a fine, high-stepping hackney!

"I suppose ye want my cart and my wood too," the carter sniveled.

"I want only the horse," the Quaker replied. "I am Jethro Coke of London, and didst thou know me, thou wouldst make thy decision quickly. Unharness the poor brute, or I may change my mind."

The carter laughed roughly and gave his whip into Jethro Coke's hands. With one eye on the gold he turned to unfasten Sham. But he was too late. A slim brown boy had come seemingly from nowhere at all and was kneeling at the horse's feet, unhitching his harness. What surprised the crowd even more was to see a tiger cat poke his head out of the boy's hood and begin to lick the horse's face.

Such a laughter and a clapping went up that it sounded more like an audience at a puppet show than a group of early-morning citizens on their way to the day's tasks.

BENJAMIN BIGGLE GOES
FOR A RIDE

THE QUAKER, JETHRO COKE, was a retired merchant who owned a parcel of land on the out-
skirts of London. The plight of the overburdened
horse had moved him to action. Now he saw a boy
who also needed help.

"At the foot of a wooded hill," he told Agba,
"I've an olden barn. It has not heard the whinny of

a horse nor the cushioned footfalls of a cat for many a year. Thou and thy cat too will be welcome there. The poor broken-down horse has need of you both."

And so, within less than a week, Sham and Agba and Grimalkin were on their way to England.

When Agba beheld the comfortable barn and the hillside pastures owned by Mister Coke, he was certain that the power of the wheat ear had spent itself.

Jethro Coke's wife was dead, and he had given the running of his household to Mistress Cockburn, a plump, motherly person who had eyes like black raisins and always a red spot on each cheek, as if she had just been bending over a hot fire.

Mistress Cockburn not only found time to roast great haunches of mutton and stir up puddings and cakes, but she waited upon Mister Coke's daughter and played nursemaid to her new baby. As for Benjamin Biggle, Mistress Cockburn set a place at table for him and nodded a stiff good morning to him with her starched cap. More than that she would not do.

"Benjamin Biggle is a fat dolt!" she told Mister Coke on more than one occasion. And while Mister

Coke was inclined, secretly, to agree with her, he tried to make the best of matters for his daughter's sake. Besides, he was a birthright Quaker, and he looked upon all God's creatures as friends.

"Benjamin," he said to his son-in-law shortly after his return from Paris, "I've a surprise for thee. Follow me."

With an expectant gleam in his eye, Benjamin Biggle followed Mister Coke down the hill to the barn. There they looked in upon a busy scene. Agba, his hood thrown back, was dyeing the white tufts of hair that had grown in on Sham's knees where he had cut them in the streets of Paris. Meanwhile Grimalkin was sitting on Sham's back, polishing his own whiskers.

"Good morning, friends," the Quaker nodded in turn to Agba and Sham and Grimalkin.

The sound of Mister Coke's voice fell pleasantly upon Sham's ears. And Agba's hands, as they applied the dye made from rootlets, felt comforting to him. He stood so still he might have been a stuffed horse in a museum.

"I bought this poor beast out of pity," Mister Coke was saying to his son-in-law. "He appears to be gaunt and bowed by years and ill use, but with the good care of this devoted boy he will fill out and make thee a nice quiet pacer."

"Aye, Papa Coke," replied Benjamin Biggle as he squared his hat over his small black wig. "Upwards of a year I have needed a horse and carriage."

The blood mounted in Mister Coke's face. For a long moment he seemed unable to speak. Then he controlled his voice with effort. "A horse, aye," he said, "but a carriage, no! A carriage is not necessary, and therefore would be a vain adornment. Pride and conceit are against my principles."

"But, Papa Coke," pleaded the son-in-law, biting his lip nervously, "I have never sat a horse!"

"Pshaw and nonsense! I can assure thee that a child could sit this sedate mount. He is just the horse for a draper like thee. In my mind's eye I can already see thee, traveling about the countryside, calling on housewives."

Benjamin Biggle's face was growing as white as a mixing of dough. He took a sidelong glance at Sham, who returned the look with a warning movement of his ears.

"It would seem best," said Mister Coke as he lifted the pocket flap of his coat and took an almanack from his pocket, "it would seem best to wait until, say, Third Month, Fourth Day. The almanack promises more settled weather then, and the little cob should be ready for a gentle canter. Shall we say the forenoon of Third Month, Fourth Day, for thy first ride?"

Benjamin Biggle sighed in relief. Third Month was a long time off. "Be it so, Papa Coke," he said brightly. Then he squinted at the position of the sun. "Mistress Cockburn is probably buttering the scones for our tea. We would better go."

Agba watched the two men walk up the hill — the long strides of Mister Coke, and the quick, rocking gait of Mister Biggle. Then he went back to work on Sham's scars.

With the coming of spring, Sham lost his starveling look. He began to appear the four-year-old that he really was. Once more his coat was burnished gold, with the course of his veins showing full and large.

Under the kind mothering of Mistress Cockburn, Agba thrived too. She filled his plate with pigeon pie and dumplings, and when she discovered that the boy had a special liking for confections, she saw to it that each day he had a goodly helping of whipped syllabub or almond cake, or perhaps an apple pasty. All the while the boy ate, Mistress

Cockburn kept up such a stream of conversation that it was scarcely any time at all before he understood such English words as: *eat, poor boy, a bit of cake, beautiful daughter, fat dolt.* Mistress Cockburn even found time to teach Agba his letters from her cookery book.

In return, he would show her the amulets in his bag and Sham's pedigree. Of course she could not read the Arabic writing, but she was tremendously impressed with its importance.

Fourth Day of Third Month dawned. In spite of the promise of the almanack, there was a fine drizzle in the air. But Jethro Coke was not one to be thwarted by weather. He saw to it that his son-in-law was up and about early. He even fitted him with an oiled cloth cover for his hat and an oiled cloth cape for his shoulders.

As Agba led Sham, all saddled and bridled, out of his stall and up the winding path to the house, the horse took one look at the flapping figure coming toward him. Then his ears went back and he jolted to a stop. He snorted at the voluminous cape of oiled cloth. He listened to the noise it made as it bellied in the wind. Benjamin Biggle must have seemed like some great monster to him. It was all

Agba could do to keep him from galloping back to the barn.

At sight of Sham, Benjamin Biggle halted too. For a full moment it looked as if his knees might buckle under his weight. If Sham was afraid of him, it was plain to see that he was twice as fearful of Sham.

"Be not unnerved, son," said Mister Coke. "It is thy oiled cloth cape that alarms the creature. Step right up."

Agba led Sham to the mounting block, then stood holding the reins.

"Come, come, Benjamin!" reasoned Mister Coke. "Let not the horse sense thy fear. Here, take the reins thyself. Now then, swing aboard!"

Shaking in fright, Mister Biggle took the reins. Then with his right hand he took hold of his left foot and tried to thrust it into the stirrup. Instead, he gave Sham a vicious jab in the ribs.

With a quick side jerk of his head, Sham turned around, knocked Mister Biggle's hat off, and sank his teeth in the man's black wig. The moment Sham tasted the pomade, however, he dropped the wig on the rain-soaked path.

Benjamin Biggle was furious. "I'll ride the beast if

109

it kills me," he said between tight lips. And donning his wig at a rakish angle, he swung his leg over Sham's back, heaved into the saddle, and grabbed the reins up short.

Like a barn swallow in flight Sham wheeled, and with a beautiful soaring motion he flew to the safety of his stall. As he dashed through the door, Benjamin Biggle was scraped off his back and into a mud puddle, where he sprawled, his breeches soaked through and the wind knocked out of his body.

As if this were not enough trouble for one day, Grimalkin pounced on his head, screamed in his face, and ruined what was left of the black wig.

That afternoon as Agba cleaned Sham's tackle, a faint sound, very much like a chuckle, escaped him every now and again. Even Grimalkin wore a smirk on his face as he perched on Sham's crest and watched Agba remove all traces of mud.

Suddenly Agba looked up to find Mister Coke, Bible in hand, standing in the doorway. His face looked lined and old. For a long time he stood quietly, and the silence was a cord between the boy and himself.

At last he spoke, using little words and short sentences so that Agba would understand. But if he had used no words at all, Agba would have known.

"Thou and thy horse and thy cat shall ever be dear to me," Mister Coke began in halting tones. "Thou must try to understand, lad."

Agba looked into the deep-set blue eyes of Mister Coke. His own eyes blurred.

"It is about my son-in-law, lad," Mister Coke went on. "He is confined to his bed from the morning's experience. He is very sore on the matter. It is his wish that the horse be sent away at once. And Hannah, who is my only daughter, pleads his cause."

Agba noticed, with a chill of fear, that all this while he had been tracing the wheat ear on Sham's chest.

Seeing the fright on the boy's face, Mister Coke put a gentle hand on his shoulder. "Come, come, lad. I am merely selling thy horse to the good Roger Williams, keeper of the Red Lion Inn. He loans out horses to merchant travelers whose mounts are travel-weary. Then, when the merchants are next in the vicinity, they return the mounts. Have no fear, lad, Roger Williams will use thy horse well. And I have the man's word that thou, and thy cat

111

too, will find a good home above the stable. He will come for thee and thy creatures early tomorrow morning."

"Now," said Mister Coke as he adjusted his square-rimmed spectacles, "let us read a verse or two from the Bible. It will help to cheer our hearts. Then I will leave thee without any words of farewell."

Standing so the light would fall over his shoulder, Mister Coke let the Bible open where it would. And suddenly the years seemed to wash away and his face was wreathed in smiles.

" 'The horse,' " he read, with gusto, " 'rejoiceth in his strength. . . . He paweth in the valley. . . . He is not affrighted. . . . He swalloweth the ground with fierceness and rage. He saith among the trumpets, Ha, Ha!' "

A look that was close to a wink ventured across Jethro Coke's face as he closed the book. Then he turned, and sprightly as a boy, leaped across the mud puddle where Benjamin Biggle had fallen.

Agba thought he heard a chuckle and then words coming back to him out of the mist: "The horse saith among the trumpets, Ha, Ha!"

AT THE SIGN OF THE RED LION

AGBA COULD HAVE BEEN HAPPY at the Red Lion
if there had been only Mister Williams, the
keeper of the inn, to consider. He was a mild-man-
nered man, with red, bushy eyebrows that traveled up and down when he spoke. And when he
smiled, as he did often, they completely hid his

eyes and gave him a sheep-dog look. Mister Williams was kindness itself.

It was Mistress Williams who made life hard. She was an enormous woman who went into hysterics every time she saw Agba. "*Mis*-ter Williams!" she would shriek at the top of her lungs. "That — that varmint-in-a-hood! Get 'im outa here! 'E gives me the creeps! It's 'im or me, I tell ye!"

The truth of the matter was that Agba's deep, searching eyes, his soft, pattering footsteps, his flowing mantle and quiet ways, were so foreign to her own coarseness that she felt ill at ease in his presence.

As for Grimalkin, the poor cat could not even cross her path without sending the woman into a fit. When one night she accidentally stepped on his tail, there was such a yowling that she insisted the cat and the boy must go that instant. And so, within less than a fortnight after they had arrived, Agba and Grimalkin were turned away from the inn without so much as an oatcake or a handful of walnuts to take along.

Mister Williams walked with Agba as far as the road. There he stopped by the lanthorn that hung from the sign of the Red Lion. Even by its feeble glow Agba could see that the man was distressed.

114

"Y' understand, lad," he said, his eyebrows working up and down with emotion, "y' understand I got me customers to think about. Mistress Williams knows an awful lot about cookery. Why, travelers come a good long ways just to taste of 'er whortleberry pie. I got to 'umor 'er, boy. You trot along now to Jethro Coke's house. 'E'll take ye in, I've no doubt of it. As for your 'orse," he added with assurance, "I paid my good money fer 'im an' I promises to use 'im well."

This he meant to do. But Mister Williams was not the man for a spirited horse like Sham. He made quick, puppetlike motions, as if his joints were controlled by strings. When he came into Sham's stall, he had a way of lunging in. Nearly always he carried some tool — a pitchfork or a hoe or a bellows. And he held it like a spear, ready for action.

The old, plodding horses in the stable were used to Mister Williams, but Sham snorted and reared every time he came near. Then the good man would try to calm the horse by giving him a grooming. But here again the man was as awkward as a pump without a handle. He knew none of the niceties of grooming. He would rub along Sham's barrel from shoulder to hip, never realizing that near the hip the hairs grew in a little swirl. This lack of skill irritated Sham, for Agba was always careful to rub his coat the way that the hairs grew.

When it came to saddling, the innkeeper had an annoying habit of dropping the saddle on Sham's back and then shoving it forward into place, thus pinching and pulling the hairs the wrong way. When a rider mounted, the torment increased.

It was not surprising that Sham resorted to all manner of tricks to get rid of the pinching saddle. He sidled along walls and trees, thus squeezing his rider's leg. He twisted his body into a cork- screw. He reared. He kicked. He balked. He threw so many guests of the Red Lion that finally Mister Williams decided he must do something about it. He called in Silas Slade, a weasel-eyed man known as the best horse-breaker in all London.

"Slade," Mister Williams said, "I hain't never seen a 'orse like this 'un. It's 'is *spirit*. 'E not only unseats the clumsy fellows like me, but the best riders in the kingdom. 'E knows 'e'll be licked fer it, but it don't matter to 'im. The only 'uman bein' what can 'andle 'im is a spindlin' boy."

"*Hmph!*" snorted Slade, his eyes gleaming. "I've yet to see the beast I couldn't break. 'E's feelin' 'is oats, 'e is. We'll get the meanness out of 'im!"

116

The first thing Mister Slade did was to saddle Sham in his expert manner and swing up. And the next thing he knew he was being carried into the inn, and a doctor was bending over him, shaking his head gravely.

When Mister Slade was poulticed and bandaged, and his leg put in a splint, he called Mister Williams to his side. "I'll break the brute yet," he said between swollen lips. "See that 'e's moved into a small stall without a window. Tie 'im so 'e can't move. Give 'im no grain and only a little water."

Agba, meanwhile, had never left the vicinity of the Red Lion. He and Grimalkin had wandered forlornly about the countryside, sleeping in hedgerows, living on what food they could pick up in woods and fields.

One moon-white night, Agba's loneliness seemed more than he could bear. He and Grimalkin were seeking shelter in a haycock. They had had nothing to eat that day, and neither of them could sleep. Grimalkin was hunting little gray field mice, and Agba was looking up at the moon, seeing Sham in its shadows.

The Sultan's words were drumming in his ears: "As long as the horse shall live . . . as long as the horse shall live . . ." He *must* get back to Sham!

He shook the straw from his mantle, swooped up Grimalkin, and ran silently through the night to the Red Lion.

As he reached the inn, he could see by the light in the taproom the bustling form of Mistress Williams. Quickly he changed his plans. Instead of approaching the stables by means of the courtyard, he would run around behind the brick wall that encircled the stables. If he scaled this wall, he could enter Sham's stall without being seen by Mistress Williams.

Agba felt like a thief, creeping along in the moon-dappled night, groping his way around the ivy-covered wall. Suddenly he stopped midway of the wall. Sham's stall, he figured, would be about opposite where he stood. He undid his turban, knotted one end, and caught it on an iron picket that jutted over the ledge of the wall. Then, with Grimalkin clinging to his shoulder, he climbed the wall and soundlessly slid down into the stable yard.

Grimalkin was everywhere at once. The familiar smells and sounds of the stable maddened him with delight. He streaked first into one stall and then another.

118

Mistress Williams at the time was in the midst of preparing porridge for tomorrow's breakfast. Suddenly she discovered that she had no salt. None at all. So she lighted a lanthorn and picked her way out to the stables where Mister Williams always kept a skipple of salt for the horses.

As she entered the stable yard, holding her lanthorn aloft, the rays of light fell upon the whirling antics of Grimalkin.

If the woman had seen a ghost, her screeching could not have been more terrible. It penetrated the inn like a bolt of lightning. Out flew Mister Williams, followed by Silas Slade on crutches, all the journeymen who had not yet gone to their beds, and a constable of the watch, brandishing his horse pistol.

Agba was frozen with fear. He could not move. His feet seemed part of the earth on which he stood. Even Grimalkin stopped in his tracks. Then with a flying leap he found the harbor of Agba's arms.

" 'E's a footpad, constable!" yelled Mistress Williams. "A 'orse thief, 'e is! Jail 'im, I beg o' ye!"

Mister Williams' eyebrows were working up and down furiously. "The boy ain't a bad one," he pleaded to the constable. " 'E comes from Morocco, and 'e's gentle as a butterfly. What's more," and he shook his head and pointed to his lips, "the boy can't say a word."

The constable took a quick look at the telltale turban hanging over the wall. Then, over the protests of Mister Williams, he clapped a pair of wrist irons on Agba and led him away to Newgate Jail.

NEWGATE JAIL

AFTER WALKING SWIFTLY FOR TWENTY MINUTES, the constable and Agba stood before a massive stone building.

"Open up!" shouted the constable. "Open up!"

"Ho! It's you, Muggins," the sentinel bawled out. "Who's the poppet in a sack yer draggin' in? What's his crime?"

While the sentinel and the constable were engaged in loud conversation, Agba's eyes were drawn to the towers and battlements with muskets trained down on him.

The moon was washing the face of the jail with cold white rays. It made Agba feel cold too. Then, in a niche in the wall, he spied the statue of a white-robed woman. Curled at her feet was a cat so like Grimalkin that he might have sat for the image. Suddenly Agba felt warm again.

The constable laughed loudly when he saw Agba looking at the wall. "Don't nobody try to scale *this* wall," he said, his teeth showing like white fangs in the moonlight. Then he jerked Agba inside a yawning entrance where a turnkey stood, holding a torch in one hand and a great ring of keys in the other. With a whishing sound, the turnkey closed the door behind them and led the way down a narrow passage.

The stone floor of the passageway was cold and clammy. Once Agba slipped, and the constable boxed his ears sharply. Agba shook in terror. He wondered if he and Sham would ever meet again, would ever thunder across the fields again, would ever feel the wind beneath the sun.

Now the turnkey stopped before an iron-bolted

door. He unlocked it with a loud jangling of keys and motioned the constable and Agba inside.

Then he went away, carefully bolting the door behind him.

Wrist and leg irons hung everywhere on the walls, and three tiny scales stood on a shelf in an open cupboard.

"This is the bread chamber," the constable announced. "The scales are to measure your bread with. You get eight ounces a day. And good enough for a horse thief!"

Soundlessly the door opened and the chief warder himself entered. He was a squat man with a tightly drawn scar on his temple. He sat down at a table, reached for a crow-quill pen and pointed it at Agba.

"Where'd ye pick it up, Muggins?"

"At the Red Lion, sir."

"Offense?"

"Horse thievin'."

"Name?"

"That I can't say, sir. The keeper of the Red Lion says he comes from Morocco. He can't talk."

A look of doubt crossed the warder's face. "Search him!"

The big hands of the constable began at Agba's

neck. They found the bag containing the amulets and Sham's pedigree. Tearing the bag from Agba's neck, the constable tossed it on the table. The amulets spilled out, making little twinkles of light. Quickly the warder scooped them into his pocket. Then he poked his fingers into the bag and pulled out the pedigree.

"Ah-ha!" he nodded, making a pretense at reading the Arabic writing. "Foul work afoot!" Fearing to show his ignorance, he tore the pedigree into little pieces and swept them to the floor.

Agba's eyes widened in horror. Sham's pedigree destroyed! But the warder was hurrying through the examination, not knowing what he had destroyed.

"What else has he got on him, Muggins?"

The constable's hands suddenly found the furry warmth of Grimalkin.

"*Pfft! Miaow! Pfft!*" Grimalkin hissed and spat and scratched.

Yelling in fright and pain, the constable grabbed Grimalkin by the tail. "Into the cistern ye go!" he shouted.

Agba's bound hands flew out in a pleading gesture. They must not take Grimalkin away! He would have no one at all to care for.

124

All at once the warder was on his feet, the pulse in the scar at his temple beating wildly. "Muggins," he whispered hoarsely, "I live in the shadow of the statue out there night and day. The cat at the dame's feet is supposed to be Dick Whittington's own cat!"

He wiped the perspiration from his brow and slumped into his chair. Agba felt a thin thread of hope. He watched the warder's face. He counted the pulse beats that showed in the scar. One — two — three — four — five — six . . .

"Who's Dick Whittington?" faltered the constable.

"Who's Dick Whittington!" the warder thundered. "Egad, man, he was thrice Lord Mayor of London. And 'twas a cat that made his fortune. 'Twas a cat he sold to the Sultan of Morocco to clean up the rats there. And 'twas the Lord Mayor himself who had the statue built." He glowered at the constable. "How dare ye offer to kill a cat? How dare ye? It's bad luck. Give it back to the boy, I tell ye."

Muggins' mouth fell open. Dazed, he handed the cat back to Agba.

"But," added the warder, suddenly ashamed of his fear, "the cat gets no bread. And eight ounces is too much for the boy. Six will do." Quickly he fastened a set of leg irons to Agba's ankles and summoned a guard who stood outside the door.

"Lock him up in the Stone Hold!" he commanded.

Dragging his heavy iron chains with every step, Agba was led away to the dungeon.

THE VISITORS' BELL

THE DAYS THAT FOLLOWED were dismal and wretched for Agba. He had nothing at all to do. Once a guard told him to clean the dungeon, but he laughed coarsely as he said it, knowing there was neither broom nor rag with which to clean.

Agba could not even move without stumbling over someone's legs or irons, and being kicked as a result. At last he crawled into a corner and sat mo-

127

tionless in a kind of dream, holding Grimalkin by the hour.

Days stretched out into weeks. He shared with Grimalkin his bread and barley gruel and the cooked-out morsel of meat which the prisoners were given once a week. Grimalkin repaid Agba's generosity. The dungeon was freer of mice and rats than was the warder's own bedchamber.

On visiting days, Agba heard the visitors' bell clang loudly again and again, followed by the scraping of chains as his prisonmates shuffled to the visitors' room. But no one ever came to see him. He and Grimalkin were left quite alone.

All this while the Quaker and his housekeeper, Mistress Cockburn, thought that Agba and Sham were happily located at the Red Lion. Busy though Mistress Cockburn was, she missed Agba's quiet ways, and one fair summer's day she decided to go to the Red Lion and take him a treat. She baked a goodly batch of sugar tarts and put them in a hamper along with some newly ripe peaches, the browned crust of a Cheshire-cheese pudding, and a few garden carrots. Then she covered the hamper with a white linen cloth and set off for the inn.

She hummed a little tune as she boarded the coach, thinking how pleased the poor boy would be to taste his favorite sugar tarts. And she was thinking, too, how his somber black eyes would light up when he saw the cleanly scrubbed carrots for his beloved Sham and the Cheshire-cheese nubbins for Grimalkin. As the coach jolted along, she kept peeking in under the white linen napkin to make sure that her tarts were not getting squashed nor the peaches bruised.

So busy was she, trying to think of little happenings to tell Agba, that she hardly noticed how fast the horses were traveling. And suddenly, far sooner than she had expected, the driver was calling out, "Cow Cross Lane at the sign of the Red Lion." She alighted as quickly as she could, brushed the dust from her bonnet, shook out the folds of her skirt, and walked briskly into the great room of the inn.

"Good day, sir," she said to a busy little man with red eyebrows. "Are you the keeper of the Red Lion?"

Mister Williams' eyebrows traveled up and down, and a pleased expression came over his face.

"That I am, my good woman," he spoke in his best manner. "A vast weight you are carrying there, I mean the hamper, madam. Pray, may I help you?"

Mistress Cockburn thanked him kindly, then

stated her business. "It is three calendar months," she said, "since a little hooded horseboy left the household of my employer, Jethro Coke. And to say the truth, sir, I have missed the poor boy sorely. If you judge it proper, sir, I should like to trot around to your stable and surprise him at his work."

Mister Williams opened his mouth to answer, but shut it quickly again, for his wife had risen up from behind the bar counter like a jack-in-the-box.

"You'll find the thief in Newgate Jail," she snapped. Then she took her broom and began sweeping her way toward Mistress Cockburn, who soon found herself out in Cow Cross Lane in front of the Red Lion.

She stood there, dazed, in the very center of the lane, unmindful that a coach-and-six was rattling toward her at a great pace. The driver had to turn sharply to avoid hitting her.

With much pulling and shouting, he halted his horses. Then the window of the coach was lowered, and the plumed head of an elderly but beautiful woman looked out.

"For your welfare, madam," spoke a silvery voice, "I pray you to step back out of the lane."

Mistress Cockburn came to with a start. "Begging your pardon," she said with a pretty curtsy,

130

"but the honestest lad I know has been sent to Newgate Jail, and I am all a-twitter."

The plumed head disappeared. There was the sound of a low-voiced conference. Then the coachman, in scarlet livery, stepped down from his box and opened the door of the coach. Out stepped a gentleman. He was powdered and bewigged like all noblemen of his day, but that was not what Mistress Cockburn noticed. What impressed Mistress Cockburn was the kindliness of his gray eyes and the courtesy with which he addressed her.

"It so happens," he was saying, "that we are on our way to Newgate now. The lady to whom you have just spoken is Her Grace, the Dowager Duchess of Marlborough."

Mistress Cockburn clapped her hand over her mouth in astonishment. Why, the Dowager Duchess of Marlborough was as much at home in Windsor Castle as the Queen herself. It was almost like meeting the Queen!

"The Duchess is my mother-in-law," the nobleman went on, "and I am the Earl of Godolphin."

Mistress Cockburn made a low curtsy, inclining her head until her nose grazed the handle of her hamper.

The Earl returned her bow. "As you mayhap

know," he said, "the Duchess oft visits the prisoners to study their cases. Since today is Visitors' Day, madam, the Duchess and I would be pleased to have your company to Newgate."

Mistress Cockburn flushed with pleasure. She was too overwhelmed to talk. So she said nothing at all, but climbed into the coach and sat facing the beautiful Duchess.

Apparently the Duchess was in a great hurry, for the driver cracked his whip and the coach went flying down the lane and on toward the heart of London. The rattle and clatter made by hooves and wheels was so great that there was no chance for conversation. Mistress Cockburn had all she could do to clutch her bonnet with one hand and her hamper with the other.

Meanwhile in the Stone Hold at Newgate Jail, Agba and Grimalkin were listening to the visitors' bell and to the sound of footsteps and chains leaving their dungeon. Finally the bell became quiet, the clanking of chains grew fainter and fainter, and their small world was sealed in silence.

Agba lay down on the meager litter of straw. Perhaps if he slept he would be lost in a dream, and the prison walls would fall away and he and Sham would be together again. Perhaps in his dream he would be grooming Sham, going over the wheat ear quickly, then lingering long on the white spot.

Presently Grimalkin hooked his paw over Agba's arm as if to attract his attention. The ponderous bolt was rasping along its iron groove. The door was coming open. A breath of air was flowing into the cell. It smelled of lavender mingled with the fragrance of freshly baked cakes.

For a few seconds the light from the corridor blinded Agba. Then his eyes went wide. There, standing on the threshold, was the chief warder, rubbing his hands and bowing like a reed in the wind. And behind him stood Mistress Cockburn with a nobleman and a lady. Mistress Cockburn's eyes were blacker than burnt raisins and her cheeks flamed. "It's him all right!" she exclaimed, bursting into tears. "Oh, my poor boy . . ."

Agba smiled at Mistress Cockburn, and such a warmth and happiness coursed through his body that he was afraid he was going to cry too.

"As I was telling ye, yer Grace," the warder was saying, "he can't talk at all. The only sounds he makes is a singsong humming, sort of like a lullaby when he and the cat beds down for the night."

"And what," asked the Duchess, "is the boy's offense?"

The pulse showing in the warder's scar was beating fast.

"As I understand it, yer Grace," he said, "the boy climbed over the wall into the stable yard of the Red Lion in the dead of night. Horse thievin' was his business."

Mistress Cockburn flew into a rage. "It's not so, yer Grace. The boy only wanted to see his horse, which he brought all the way from Africa. And he himself wears the story of the horse in a little bag around his neck. Show it to the lady and gentlemen, Agba."

Agba's hand went to his neck. He shook his head.

The warder hesitated, then spoke. "Yer Grace, the lady says the truth. The boy *was* wearin' a bag around his neck, and the constable he . . . he . . ."

"He what?" demanded the Earl.

"Well, the papers is gone, my Lord, but I'll give him the bag with the amulets in it."

He took the bag from his pocket, and with a false show of kindness tied it about the boy's neck.

"My poor boy! My poor boy!" Mistress Cockburn said over and over. Then she opened her hamper and placed a tart in Agba's hand. She gave Grimalkin a crust of Cheshire-cheese cake, and quickly covered the basket to hide the brightly scrubbed carrots.

Agba bit into the delicious tart. He longed to tell Mistress Cockburn — in words she had taught him from her own cookery book — how good it tasted. But all he did was to eat and smile through his tears.

"I cannot help tumbling out my thoughts," the Duchess was saying to the Earl in her tinkling, music-box voice. "My life is very near run out, and my only pleasure is doing good. Let us inquire into this case, and if it prove a worthy one, why could not . . ."

She flashed a radiant smile upon the Earl, and left her words fluttering in mid-air.

The Earl of Godolphin caught up her sentence and finished it off. "And if his case proves worthy," he said quietly, "I will want him to help in my stables at Gog Magog. By all that is good and holy, I promise it!"

Agba looked up quickly. It was plain to see that he had a question to ask.

The Earl of Godolphin chuckled deep down in his throat. "Be eased of your fears," he said. "We will go at once to the Red Lion to buy your horse. He will be welcome at Gog Magog. And the cat too. There is room for all."

THE GREEN HILLS OF GOG MAGOG

T HAT SAME FAIR SUMMER'S DAY, Sham was lying in his stall at the Red Lion. He no longer
needed to be shackled. No one feared him any
more. He was too weak to kick and charge.

For weeks he had lived in a kind of daze, willing
to lie on his bed of straw and let the world go on
about him. Over the half-door of his stall he could

136

hear the rattle of pewter cups in the inn and listen to the comings and goings of horses and journeymen. He caught the mingled smell of dust and sweat when the horses came in. He caught the rain smells and heard the first drops beat out a mournful medley on the roof over his head. He snuffed the winds. But he was no longer a part of the smells and the sounds.

Mister Williams shook his head sadly every time he passed Sham's stall. "That there 'orse, 'e's got a gnawin' pull inside 'im. 'E's missin' that boy."

On this summer's afternoon, the sound made by Mistress Williams banging her pots and pans was suddenly muffled by the thunder of hooves and the rumble of wheels.

Lying half awake, half asleep, Sham heard the other horses in their stalls neigh a greeting to the newcomers. He heard the high, scrabbling voice of Mistress Williams. Then a silence broken by many footsteps and the low laughter of a gentlewoman.

The next thing he knew the door of his stall was thrown open, a feather-light creature was by his side, and a boy's slim brown fingers were stroking his neck.

Sham touched Agba's cheek with his feelers, as if to make sure of him. Then an excited whicker escaped him. He lipped the boy. He swiped his cheek with a great pink tongue. He tasted the warm, salty tears. Then he neighed his happiness to the whole wide world.

Thrusting his forefeet in front of him, he struggled to his feet. Lying down was no way to greet friends! He shuddered the straw from his coat, as if to apologize for his lack of grooming.

A change came over him. He snorted at the half-circle of people about him, at the handsome gentleman in wine-colored velvet, at the lady in silk and gold lace, at the innkeeper and his wife standing at a respectful distance.

His eyes came back to Agba. "Let us be off!" he seemed to say. "Somewhere. *Anywhere!*"

The Earl of Godolphin laughed in agreement. Then he exchanged a few quiet words with Mister Williams, and the arrangements to buy Sham were quickly made. In no time at all Agba and Grimalkin were mounted on Sham, while a gathering of all the chance droppers-in at the Red Lion gawped curiously at the coach-and-six, and at the hooded boy and the tiger cat who sat a well-mannered bay horse.

Mister Williams' eyebrows were traveling up and down at a great rate. "Split my windpipe!" he said to a journeyman who had once been tossed off by Sham, "it hain't the same beast, I tell ye! 'E hain't stubborn nor vicious at all. 'E and the boy are all of one color and all of one mind. They can't wait to go! D'you know," he exclaimed, slapping the man on the back, "that 'orse — 'e's got *brains!*"

The Earl leaned his head out of the coach window. "We will lead the way up to Gog Magog," he called to Agba. "Our pace will be slow to accommodate the weakened condition of your mount." And he smiled a little smile of encouragement.

If the road to the hills of Gog Magog had been the road to the garden of heaven, the three silent creatures could not have been happier. It seemed as if the green meadows and the woodlands and clear streams had been created for them alone. The sun warmed their backs. The wind blew for their pleasure. They sucked it deep into their lungs. It washed them free.

Agba was almost sorry when the driver of the coach pulled to a stop before a gate surmounted by the crest of a dolphin. He wished the ride could go on forever.

The Duchess, however, seemed glad the journey was over.

"I declare, my lad," she sighed, leaning her head wearily against the gilded frame of the coach window, "you and your mount and your kitling appear fresher than when you started."

Now the gate was opened by two men in livery, and the coach-and-six led the way over a bridge and up a gentle hill between yews and hawthorn trees to the stables of the Earl of Godolphin.

Agba could not believe his eyes. It was the stable, not the house, that crowned the hill, and there was a stream encircling the hill where mares and their foals were drinking. He jumped to his bare feet. The turf was soft and springy. The green grass tickled up between his toes. He touched Sham's white spot with his toe. The white spot! The white spot! Here at last Sham could fulfill the promise it held.

Grimalkin, who had settled into the saddle in great dignity, now cuffed Agba with his paw, as much as to say, "Mind your manners, the Earl is headed this way."

Agba stood at attention, but he could not keep his shining eyes from gathering in the whole scene:

the long range of box stalls opened to the south sun, the shady paddock, the park for a training ground. Why, there were no walls anywhere! Only green hedges afar off, where the meadows came to an end. And rows of elm trees brushing the clouds. And willows trailing their fingers in the stream.

An exercise boy came into the yard with a string of running horses. Their haunches gleamed in the sun.

Agba drew a quick breath. Soon Sham's coat would be sleek and shining too. Soon Sham would be the wind beneath the sun. Soon he would be showing his gratitude to the Earl, winning races, bringing honor to Gog Magog.

Agba's thoughts were cut short. A spidery man with a waggish air about him was presenting himself to the Earl of Godolphin.

"A very g-g-good morning, your Lordship," he stuttered. And as he bowed he took an appraising look at the underfed horse, the strangely dressed boy, and the tiger cat sitting the horse with a superior grin.

The Earl of Godolphin followed his glance.

"Twickerham," he said, "I have brought you a new horseboy, and this is his little bay stallion. Ill luck has dogged their footsteps. They have traveled a hard road and a long one. From henceforward they will be in your charge."

For only an instant a cloud darkened the groom's face. "Very g-good, your Lordship," he said.

The Earl dismissed the coach and turned to Agba. "I once read a novel laid in Morocco," he said. "The characters had curious names — curious to me, of course. There was El Hayanie and Hamed O Bryhim, and one was Agba. Since I have to call you by some name, I shall choose the shortest one: Agba. I desire you to give me your opinion of this name by the strength of your handclasp."

With his head groom standing by in open-mouthed amazement, the Earl of Godolphin, son of the Lord Treasurer of England, held out his hand to Agba. The small brown hand and the long-fingered white one met, and there was such a wringing clasp between them that the Earl's face broke into a great smile. Agba smiled too. If only the Earl knew! He had chosen the name that was already the boy's own.

"Agba," he said, "you will be in the care of my head groom, Mister Titus Twickerham. He is breeder and trainer for the Gog Magog stables. I hope and pray that you will be happy."

Agba bowed first to the Earl and then to the groom, blinking hard to keep away the tears of happiness.

The Earl of Godolphin now cleared his throat and fingered his neck cloth a trifle uneasily. "Twickerham," he hesitated, "what think you of the merits of the stallion?"

The groom searched the Earl's face, trying to read his feelings there. Seeing only an open countenance, he rocked back and forth on his heels in importance. Then he approached Sham's head. Instantly Sham nosed the sky. Mister Twickerham reached for the bridle. He tried to force Sham's head down, but it was only with Agba's help that he could look into the horse's mouth. He tried to lift a hoof, but Sham's legs were pillars driven into the earth. Yet with only a feather touch, Agba lifted a foot as easily as if it were Grimalkin's paw.

Red of face, Titus Twickerham stepped back. He measured the horse with his eyes. From withers to hoof. From withers to tail. Again and again he measured. He noted the scars on the horse's knees. Then he pursed his lips.

"Your L-lordship," he began, "this-here beast would be the laughing stock at the race-c-c-course. He's not lusty enough to endure the distances. With the b-best care in the kingdom he'd still be a broken-kneed cob. *And!*" here Mister Twickerham pointed a thin forefinger, while his face gave out the faintest suggestion of a sneer, "if your Lordship will k-kindly note the height of the crest, he will see 'tis almost a deformity.

"To *my* mind," he concluded, enjoying the importance of the moment, "this ain't a running horse, and d-d-don't let nobody tell your Lordship that he'd make a good sire, either. Colts with him for a father would be violent-tempered and weedy as c-c-cattails."

The Earl of Godolphin did not change expression. For long seconds he stood perfectly still. "If this be true," he said at last, "feed him until he loses his gaunt look. Then we'll see what's to be done with him. Perhaps he can work the machine that pumps water into the fish pond."

Agba looked at the Earl aghast. Was Sham, the pride of the Sultan's royal stables, never to have a chance to prove himself? Was he always to be a work horse?

144

HOBGOBLIN

AGBA'S DISAPPOINTMENT was a cloud over his head. Sometimes when he rode Sham, the cloud seemed to lift and take wing for a few hours. But as he dismounted it settled on his shoulders again, enveloping him like his own black and ragged mantle.

He tried to push the cloud away with the thought that Sham was being restored to health. Here were oats and corn and hay in plenty. But whenever Titus Twickerham urged Agba to feed Sham more liberally, Agba knew the groom had but one thought in mind. He was eager to see Sham in the humble role of work horse.

And so the cloud persisted. It was there even when the Duchess of Marlborough visited the stables, bringing with her loaves of sugar for Sham, a beef kidney for Grimalkin, and a gift for Agba too. On one occasion the Duchess invited Agba into her two-wheeled chaise to present a race calendar to him. In a voice that was more like song than talk, she read to him, pointing out a few easy words such as "horse," "bay," "colt," "post."

She promised to order for him a new mantle woven from goat's hair. "It will be as fine as the mantle worn by the Sultan himself," she smiled.

Agba tried to repay her kindness by washing and polishing her chaise and by doing well whatever jobs Titus Twickerham asked of him.

There was only one duty that Agba disliked, and he disliked it with such an intensity that the blood pounded hotly through him all the while he did it. It was the cleaning of Hobgoblin's stall.

146

Hobgoblin was a big and, to Agba's way of thinking, a coarsely made stallion. He was as unlike Sham as a bull is unlike a stag. Yet Hobgoblin was king of Gog Magog, and his stall a palace. The walls were padded thickly with the fuzz of cattails covered over with leather, so that Hobgoblin would not mar the sleekness of his hide nor the perfection of his tail. The floor was laid with chalk and abundantly strewn with straw which Agba had to change three times a day. A manger of wood was not good enough for Hobgoblin. His was of marble. As for his blankets, they were emblazoned with the Earl of Godolphin's own crest. Even his fly sheets bore the crest.

"Hobgoblin's th-th-the Earl's star o' hope, Hobgoblin is," Titus Twickerham told Agba one rainy day when they were both in his stall. "Flowing in this-here stallion's veins is the p-p-purplest blood in the k-k-kingdom."

The groom stopped to wipe out the corner of Hobgoblin's eye with a clean pocket handkerchief, then went on. "The Earl — he's g-got his heart set on Hobgoblin. Through this-here stallion he's got hopes to b-breed the best line o' horses not only in the kingdom but in the world."

147

Agba preferred to listen to the drumming of the rain, but the groom's voice rose above it.

"Right this m-minute, whilst we're standin' here, the Earl is lookin' for a mare worthy of Hobgoblin. *Now*," he said, rapping his knuckles on Agba's head, "now ye understand why Hobgoblin's stall is finer th-th-than yer runt's. Hobgoblin's king of Gog Magog, he is!"

After that, whenever Agba pitched the old straw out of Hobgoblin's stall and laid in the new, his lips were set in a firm line. He hated Hobgoblin. Hated the bigness of him. Hated his powerful legs and hindquarters. Hated the fat sleekness of him. But most of all he hated Hobgoblin's eye. It had no brilliance at all. Only a sleepy look, except when the animal was aroused. Then it showed a white ring.

"Here is where Sham should be," Agba thought with every thrust of his fork. "Purple blood, indeed! Sham's ancestors came from the stables of the Prophet himself!"

One day, soon after the groom had explained Hobgoblin's importance, Gog Magog seethed with excitement. The Earl of Godolphin made frequent visits to Hobgoblin's stall. Usually his gait was dignified and his bearing stately, but this day his steps were quick and his words clipped short.

As for Titus Twickerham, he was so nervous that he could not control his stammering.

"Y-y-y-you, Ag-g-g-ba. Y-you lay a fresh l-l-litter of st-st-straw in the new m-m-mare's stall. And w-w-wash out the mang-g-g-ger. Then p-p-put in a measure of wheat b-b-bran. The mare Lady Roxana arrives t-t-t-today."

The excited pitch of Mr. Twickerham's voice when he said "Lady Roxana" made Agba bite his lips. It was the very tone he used in speaking of Hobgoblin. *Lady Roxana! Hobgoblin! Hobgoblin! Lady Roxana!* The names rankled in the boy's mind. He hated them both. Without even seeing Roxana, he knew she would be fat and sway-backed and ugly.

As Agba prepared the mare's stall, he saw the Earl and a dozen noblemen come down to the paddock. They walked about, talking in hushed, expectant voices, twirling their riding rods, taking pinches of snuff, sneezing lightly.

Suddenly a cry went up from the grooms. " 'Ere she comes! 'Ere she comes!"

Agba flew out of the stall. He made field glasses

of his fists. He strained his eyes down the lane. But the late-afternoon sun blinded him. At first he saw nothing at all. Only the hawthorn trees and the yews, standing dark and still.

Then all at once he could make out a blur of motion. It cleared. It became a shiny red van drawn by two dapple-grays.

The grays were clattering over the bridge now, and up the hill between the yews and hawthorns. They were nearing the stables. The driver, an enormous man in red livery, was drawing rein. As the horses jammed to a stop, a lackey hopped down from his perch beside the driver and went around to the back of the van. He let down the tail gate. Then, bowing from the waist, he handed a leading string to the Earl's head groom.

"Lady Roxana, daughter of The Bald Galloway!" His voice boomed out as if he were announcing a princess at a ball.

The noblemen and all the horseboys waited tensely. Titus Twickerham looked to the Earl of Godolphin with questioning eyebrows. The Earl nodded. And so, bristling with importance, the spidery figure of the groom led Lady Roxana down the ramp and into the paddock. Slowly, gently, as

150

if he were unveiling a statue, he lifted her hood and threw off her scarlet blanket.

An awed silence fell over the little company. Then, as though the wall of a dike had given way, there was a torrent of noise. Jeweled hands broke into spontaneous applause. Every voice shouted in admiration.

The Earl of Godolphin laughed aloud. Here, at last, was the answer to his dream!

Except for her tail, which was a smoky plume, Roxana was the shininess of white marble in the sun. And she wore no housings at all, only a halter made of silken rope, and across the browband were tiny rosettes of blue satin.

Roxana pawed the springy turf. She seemed glad that the jolting, jarring ride was over. A high whinny escaped her.

Suddenly there was an answering whinny, so shrill and joyous it sent shivers racing up and down Agba's spine.

"Aha!" spoke up one of the noblemen. "Hobgoblin is already welcoming his mate."

A smile played about Agba's lips. The whinny of welcome had come, *not* from Hobgoblin, but from Sham.

For a full moment Roxana alerted. Her head went up, her tail went up, her ears pricked. The noblemen gasped. If Roxana had been beautiful before, she was a living statue now.

Agba's heart melted. He had intended to hate Roxana, but all the hate was washed away.

"What symmetry!" exclaimed the Duke of Bridgewater.

"She is built like a fawn!" cried Lord Villiers.

"Aye. Exquisitely made," said the Earl of Marmaduke.

Agba scarcely heard their remarks. Way down at the end of the stables he saw Sham's head thrust out. He watched Roxana toss her mane at him, like a girl tossing her curls. He heard her whinny, this time softer, fuller, than the last.

Now there were two answers. The deep, grunting neigh of Hobgoblin and the ecstatic bugling of Sham.

"Twickerham," the Earl spoke tensely, "Hobgoblin shall meet his mate. Have him brought out."

Again the paddock was bathed in stillness. It was so quiet that Agba could hear a leaf drifting lazily to earth. A goldfinch flew overhead in yellow arcs, spinning a thin thread of song.

Titus Twickerham's words rang in Agba's ears. *A mare worthy of Hobgoblin.* That overfed monster! Agba could stand the unfairness no longer. He ran to Sham's stall. He threw wide the door. Out streaked a tongue of golden fire. It was Sham, trumpeting to the skies, Sham tasting his freedom with a wild leap. He overtook Hobgoblin being led out of his stall. He whirled around and challenged the king of Gog Magog. Hobgoblin jerked his head into the air, breaking the catch of his lead rope. For one deathly still moment the two stallions faced each other. Then they charged, the noisy thudding of their bodies lost in savage screams.

The grooms were benumbed, stupefied. For seconds they were unable to move. Then they all began running at once, getting in each other's way, throwing bucketfuls of water at the furious stallions. It was useless — like trying to smother a forest fire with hearth brooms. The air crackled and ripped with the sound of flailing hooves and snorts and shrieks.

Sham was little and quick. His legs were steel rods. He danced on them, making fierce thrusts. Hobgoblin was like a great war horse beside Sham. Now he swung his lumbering body around and gave a tremendous kick with all the power of his hindquarters.

Agba saw Sham drop down on the ground to miss the blow. In a second he was up again, spinning around to face Hobgoblin, beating at him with his flinty hooves. He saw Sham open wide his mouth and use his strong young teeth, not to bite, but to hammer with. The blows seemed no heavier than hailstones to Hobgoblin. Yet they maddened him into a wild rage. He lunged, baring his teeth, ready to sink them into Sham's neck.

With a mighty cry, Sham tossed his head upward, catching Hobgoblin under the jaw, actually lifting him up on his hind feet. The little horse rained blow upon blow on Hobgoblin, forcing him farther and farther up on his hind legs until finally he fell over backward, thrashing and kicking.

Agba beat his fists together. The great Hobgoblin was down! The massive, heaving, hulking body was grunting in pain and defeat.

A ringing cry of victory burst from Sham. With a rush he sought Lady Roxana. He leaped about her, prancing lightly as if his legs were set on springs. He arched his magnificent neck. He plumed his tail. His eyes were bold, his body wet and shining. Sham, the fleet of foot, the pride of the Sultan's stables, was on parade before the beautiful Roxana.

Suddenly they were together, touching each other with their noses, talking in excited little nickers. Then, manes and tails in flowing motion, they streaked to the far end of the paddock. It seemed plain to Agba that both Sham and Roxana wanted to be far away from the distasteful, groaning Hobgoblin.

Agba wanted to sing for joy. He longed to talk, to laugh, to cry. His hands flew to his throat helplessly. But it was Roxana whose voice substituted for his own. It was her whinny, high and joyful, that said all he wanted to say.

WICKEN FEN

AFTER A MOMENT OF STUNNED SILENCE, the Earl of Godolphin led his guests away. Twicker-ham ran to Hobgoblin, rolled him onto his belly and helped him rise. When the horse was once more in his stall, the groom followed the Earl. He must have orders before he saw Agba.

Agba, meanwhile, had gone back to work to avoid showing his joy. Not until darkness closed in did he realize what he had done. Then the gravity of it struck him. He had acted without orders. He had allowed Sham to fight Hobgoblin. Sham might have killed the Earl's favorite stallion, his star of hope!

The boy swallowed hard. He had hurt the kindliest friend he had ever had. He was ready to take whatever punishment might come.

So it was with no surprise that, as he stood in Sham's stall, he saw coming toward him the quick, spidery legs of Titus Twickerham. They cast long, frightening shadows because of the lanthorns which the groom held in each hand.

"Agba!" he called out as soon as he was within hearing. "What I has to say can be said *over* the door."

There was not the slightest hesitation or stammering in Mister Twickerham's speech. It was as if he had wound up his words in a ball and now had only to unwind them.

"The Earl wants to be quit of ye," he pronounced. "He don't want nobody ever again to mention ye or yer horse in his presence. He can't trust himself to look at ye. Not ever. Not ever, do ye hear?"

Agba bent his head. He could understand. He thought of the wheat ear, and unconsciously began tracing the swirling hairs on Sham's chest.

"Look me in the eye, ye blockhead! Take yer fingers off o' that weed. Listen sharp! All yer nag is fit for is cat's meat. Yet his Lordship says ye're to saddle him immejate and follow the North Star 'til it brings ye to Upware Inn. Get a-goin' with that saddle!"

Agba went for the saddle. His hands were shaking as he laid it on Sham's withers and slid it into place. Sham stretched his neck in Mister Twickerham's direction, opened wide his mouth, bared his teeth, and let forth a high and mighty neigh.

"Kill-devil!" the groom spat. "Laugh all ye want to now. Ye an' yer hooded turtle of a boy, and yer cat too, is going to Wicken Fen. And there, in the dismal swampland, ye're going to end out yer days."

Agba felt a chill. The night mist was rising. It reminded him of the dank air of Newgate Jail.

"Shiverin' in yer timbers, be ye, Agba?" taunted the groom. "Ye an' yer high-soundin' book name! Now we'll see if it'll help ye to follow directions.

158

When ye comes to Upware Inn, ye'll see letters written on the gable of it. They spell out: 'Five Miles from Anywhere. No Hurry.'"

Titus Twickerham scratched his head. "Huh!" he exclaimed. "Maybe ye can't read any more'n ye can talk. But no matter. Ye can't miss the inn if ye follow the North Star. Then ye turn right fer five miles an' ye'll come upon . . ." here the groom poked his head close to Agba's and let the words whistle through his teeth, "an' ye'll come upon Wicken Fen! And there, in the miry bog, ye'll find a ghostlike hovel waitin' just for ye."

Agba's hands had suddenly grown icy. It was all he could do to buckle Sham's girth strap. But at last he stood ready, taking nothing in his saddlebag but Sham's rub-rag and a spool toy which the Duchess had given Grimalkin.

"His Lordship is far too kind to ye," muttered the groom as he opened the door of the stall. "He says fer me to fasten a lanthorn to each o' yer stirrups. Then ye won't fall into the dykes and get drownt. Though, to my mind, 'twould be good riddance of all of ye. Then I wouldn't have to be sending ye barley and oats every fortnight like I'm ordered to."

He came so close now that his coarse hair

scratched Agba's face. "Fer me," his voice rasped, "I'd sooner be buried alive as spend one night in the fen country."

Grimalkin began yowling nervously. He leaped onto Mister Twickerham's head and from there to Sham's saddle. From the height of Sham's back he looked down on the groom, as much as to say, "A mounting block! That's all *ye* are!"

The groom made a wry face at the cat. "Humpf," he scoffed. "Ye an' yer mute friends be nothin' but fen slodgers!"

Now Agba swung up on Sham, and together the three creatures went out into the night.

Life was hard in the fenland, even though Titus Twickerham carried out the Earl's orders. When the roads were passable, he sent barley and oats by a peasant farmer, who delivered his load and drove off as fast as his horse would take him.

After he had gone, Agba would light a peat fire and make barley gruel for all to share.

Sometimes Agba speared for eels and pike in a crooked stream. But he was clumsy, as he had nothing but a sharp stick for a spear. Besides, the coarse sedge grass along the streams was razor-sharp, and it cut Agba's arms and legs until he had to bind them with strips from his turban. So it was not often that he and Grimalkin enjoyed the delicacy of fresh fish.

Titus Twickerham had told the truth about Wicken Fen, Agba thought in the long nights when the wind moaned and the owls hooted. It *was* dismal ground.

In winter, a white wilderness of snow walled the three creatures inside their hovel. Then Agba's mind flew back to all the promises he had made Sham, and his eyes would search Sham's to catch the faintest mistrust in their purple depths.

The only answer he got was Sham's lips nibbling along his neck. "We're in this together," he said in his own way. "Fen slodgers, all three of us!" Then with a nervous foreleg he would paw the floor of the hut, as if he wanted to be out in the howling gales. Agba would lift the hoof and feel the soundness of it — the hard wall, the cushiony frog. "See!" he would tell himself. "Sham is well and strong. The power of the wheat ear cannot last." And he laughed to feel the good warm shagginess of Sham's coat and the length of his own hair.

Winter spent itself, and spring came, scattering windflowers among the spare blades of grass. Sham rolled and rolled, trying to rub off his heavy winter coat. And when he stood up, he left great bunches of his hair lying on the grass. As soon as his back was turned, thrushes and finches and starlings picked up the hair and lined their nests with it.

Another year passed. And in all that time Agba saw but one human creature beside the peasant farmer. This one called himself a wild-fowler because he trapped ducks and geese. He looked curiously out of his birdlike eyes at the three castaways. Then he shook his head and went his way, as if he liked his own company better.

The wild creatures of Wicken Fen, however, accepted Sham and Agba and Grimalkin. Butterflies grazed Sham's nose, leaving the powder from their wings as a token of trust. And Agba made a friend of a hooded crow. One minute the crow was an earthy creature perched on his shoulder. The next he was an arrow piercing the sky.

Wicken Fen was not always drear. There were fair days when, just at sunset, Agba and Grimalkin would ride Sham along a grassy causeway to a watering place. It was more like flying than riding, for Sham no longer wore shoes, and the sound of his hooves was muted by the grass. They seemed one creature, these three, flying into the sunset.

Then they drank with the wild things, the deer and the mallards and the gulls.

One day when Agba was repairing the thatched roof of his hovel, he looked off into the distance and noticed a cloud of dust rising. It was not just a puff. It was a long, extended cloud, as if made by many horses.

He slid down the roof, glancing around quickly for Sham. There, only a few rods away, he was cavorting and kicking his heels like a colt. The boy ran to him and led him inside the hovel, closing the door securely. As he stepped out again, he almost stumbled over Grimalkin. Quickly Agba sent the cat inside too. Then he stood before the door, barricading it with his arms. He felt no fear for himself, but a nameless fear for Sham clutched at his heart.

He squinted his eyes against the sun. Now he could make out a van drawn by a pair of horses and attended by a whole cavalcade of outriders. They were coming toward him.

He could see the van clearly now. It was shiny red. The very same van in which Roxana had arrived at Gog Magog! And perched on the driver's box was Titus Twickerham!

Mister Twickerham waved his hat in the air.

163

Then he drew up with a flourish. The horsemen leaped to their feet.

"Ho th-th-there, l-l-lad," the groom stammered excitedly, as he strode toward Agba. "We have c-c-come for ye and the horse." Suddenly he realized that Agba was alone. His face went white. "The horse," he asked, "he has not d-d-d —"

Sham let out a shrill whinny just then. The color came back to Mister Twickerham's face. "L-l-lad," he spoke in sugared tones, "ye remember the m-m-mare they call R-R-Roxana?"

Agba nodded, his heart beating fast.

"W-w-well, my boy, one morning 'long about a year ago, I c-come to look at her, and b-b-bless my soul if she ain't hiding a little horse-colt by her side." Mister Twickerham came a step closer. "*And,*" he smiled, showing the gaping space in his teeth, "that little c-c-colt was the spit image o' yer horse!"

Agba looked to the other horsemen, as if he could not believe the groom's words.

" 'E speaks the truth," laughed one. "Don't 'e, lads?"

"Aye! That he does!"

Agba's heart warmed. If only he could see Sham's colt!

164

" 'Course, the Earl — he hated the sight of the colt," the groom went on, "so he named him Lath, because he was that skinny. And he says to me, 'Twickerham, just let *that one* grow. Don't ye bother to train him.' "

The coach horses began pawing the grass. Mister Twickerham ordered his assistants to take off their headstalls so they could graze.

"And now, Agba," smiled the groom, "hark to this: Lath is r-r-rising two, and yesterday when the other two-year-olds was bein' timed around the ring, Lath was watching from the p-paddock. Then what do ye calculate happened?"

Agba's eyes asked the question.

"Well, that Lath, he j-j-jumps the fence and starts racing around the ring on his own, and he catches up with the horses ahead o' him and he overtakes 'em, and he travels like a b-b-bullet until he's ahead of 'em all! And some of the two-year-olds was m-m-months older than Lath, and couldn't none o' 'em catch him."

Agba could scarcely contain his excitement. He had but one question in his mind, and the groom answered it as if it had been spoken.

"Aye, boy. By some chance his Lordship sees the whole p-p-performance, and his eyes p-p-pop so

far out o' his head I coulda hooked 'em with my bootjack. 'T-T-T-Twickerham,' he says slow-like, trying to hide his feelings, 'Twickerham,' he says, 'I was wrong. M-m-maybe Agba's little Arabian horse *is* the one to sire a new and noble b-b-breed of horses. Fetch him home, Twickerham! Home!'"

Titus Twickerham's face stretched in a grin. "So here we are, l-l-lad, waiting to take yer stallion home in t-t-triumph. And for *ye*, there's a snowy white mantle and turban what the Duchess sent along. It c-c-come all the way from Morocco."

A few minutes later Sham, wearing a blanket for the first time in two years, was loaded into the shiny red van while Grimalkin sat perched on his back, a satisfied grin on his face. Agba stood at the back of the van, looking out between the well-padded stakes. He heard the crack of the whip. He felt the floor quiver beneath his feet. He saw the splendid outriders in their red jackets move into position. He stooped down and pressed his hand against Sham's white spot.

At last Sham was being honored according to his merits! At last things were as they ought to be!

On to Gog Magog!

GOD'S DOWNS

THE EARL OF GODOLPHIN HIMSELF was waiting to welcome Sham back to Gog Magog. And he led the way, not to Sham's old stall, but to Hobgoblin's! Hobgoblin's name was no longer above the door. There were many letters there now. Agba studied them out.

168

T-H-E G-O-D-O-L-P-H-I-N A-R-A-B-I-A-N
they spelled. Why, the Earl had given Sham his
own name! A royal name! Agba wanted to wring
the Earl's hand, but a horseboy could not take such
liberties. And just as his mind was casting wildly
about for a way to thank him, the Earl himself put
out his hand.

Agba placed his palm with all its horny little
calluses within the cushioned white one of the
Earl. But it was the Earl's fingers that tightened in
a clasp so firm it made the boy blink. They stood so
for a long moment. Then the Earl cleared his
throat. "Godolphin means *God's Downs*," he said,
swallowing strangely. "And here, on God's Downs,
your Arabian will live out his days. Come, Agba,
persuade him to enter his new quarters."

Sham looked little and comical in Hobgoblin's
big stall, but he accepted it as if it were his right.
He rubbed his tail against the thickly padded walls
and sidled along them as if he found the softness
exactly to his taste.

And wonder of wonders, he saw the Lady Roxana again! They came at each other with such joyous greetings that the sound of their reunion must
have carried to Wicken Fen. Roxana did not seem

to notice that Sham's coat was shaggy and coarsened. And Sham seemed unaware that Roxana was no longer the delicate little filly he had known. She was a brood mare now, and her bones were well furnished.

"Not since the day they met have I heard a whinny so jubilant," the Earl remarked to Agba.

Life now settled down to a pleasant pace. Sham had his own private paddock, and from it he could view everything that went on about him. Twice in the year that followed he saw his son, Lath, leave Gog Magog for the great races at Newmarket. He had no idea that Lath was the pride and toast of Newmarket, but each time he welcomed the young horse home with a deep-throated neigh.

When Roxana presented Sham with Cade, a second son, Sham sniffed noses with him and nibbled along the little fellow's high crest. It seemed almost as if he were pleased and proud at having sired him! Grimalkin sniffed him, too; then wrinkled his nose as if he much preferred his own stablemate. Besides, his bones were growing old and he liked the comfort of the Godolphin Arabian's bed.

Sham's third son was born a year after Cade. They named him Regulus, and he, like Lath and

Cade, had the same high crest and the finely drawn legs of his sire.

One day when Regulus was two years old, the Earl of Godolphin summoned Agba to his house. It was the first time in all these years that Agba had ever been inside the stately brick mansion. He crossed the threshold in awe. A servant showed him to the library where, in spite of the pleasant day, the Earl was seated before a crackling fire.

"Sit down, gentle friend," the Earl said, indicating a leather hassock opposite him.

Agba was not accustomed to sitting anywhere but on the ground. Timidly he circled the hassock, like a dog settling down for a nap. Then he bent forward and seated himself gingerly. When he realized that he was not going to topple off, he crossed his legs beneath him and waited for the Earl to speak.

The Earl's face looked pinched and tired. He seemed preoccupied, as if he had forgotten Agba's presence. Absently he reached for a pair of tongs, plucked a glowing coal from the fire and lighted his pipe with a hand that was not steady.

Agba turned his eyes away. He tried to observe the room, so that he might take away a picture memory of it. But suddenly, wherever he looked, the symbols of the wheat ear and the white spot flashed before his eyes. He thought he saw them on the backs of the books that lined the walls, in the wisps of smoke the Earl blew, in the dancing flames. The signs of success and of failure! He had almost forgotten them. Now they seemed everywhere at once. Agba longed to run out of the house to see if Sham was in trouble, but the quiet and the smoke were entwining themselves about his throat, choking him. And just when he seemed unable to take another breath, the Earl spoke.

"King Charles," he began, "used to say of my father that he was never in the way, never out of the way. That," he said with a direct gaze, "is my feeling for you."

Agba's eyes were fixed on the Earl's face.

"It is right that you should know what I am about to say, Agba, for to your stallion may go the honor of improving the English race horse. Already the swiftness and the vitality of your golden Arabian are showing up in his colts. Had it not been for you, Agba, I might have discarded the purest blood of the Orient."

Agba knew that in spite of these momentous words something was wrong. He waited tensely.

172

"The news that I am a poor man," the Earl said at last, "may come as a shock to you. I have naught in this world but a title."

Agba's mouth fell open. His glance darted to the polished parquetry floor, to the shining silver sconces with branching lights, to the gardener trimming the hedge outside the window.

"Aye," the Earl nodded. "Vast estates require vast reservoirs of money. I am in low circumstances, and my debts grow clamorous. Pastures must needs be limed and rolled and harrowed, horses shod, farriers paid. Agba," he paused, then went on falteringly, "on the very eve when we are improving the strain of the English horse, I may have to let our stables and pastures for farming purposes."

The words fell with a thud. The gold clock on the mantel tolled the hour. A log split open, sent up a shower of sparks, then fell among the ashes.

For seconds the Earl stared into the fire. Then a flicker of hope lighted his eyes. "There is a three-day race meeting at Newmarket this spring," he said, "with the Queen's Plate as the prize. Should Lath or Cade or Regulus win, there would be no need to let the property. The Queen's Plate is a purse of one thousand guineas!"

The blood quickened in Agba's veins. He almost fell off the hassock in his excitement. He waited for the Earl's next words. They came in a rush.

"It is not often," he said, "that a stallion has three great sons in one race meet. Since the Godolphin Arabian is too old to compete, I am of the opinion that he should be present at Newmarket to watch the performance of Lath and Cade and Regulus. What think you of this?"

The Earl searched Agba's face, and when he read the hope and pride there, he threw back his head and laughed deeply.

THE QUEEN'S PLATE

NEWMARKET! The word set Agba on fire. Since first he had come to England he had heard horseshoers, jockeys, water boys, exercise men, saddlers, capmakers, whipmakers, the Earl, and even the Duchess say the word as if it held ice and flame in its syllables.

Now that he knew all three of Sham's sons were to run on this famous course, Agba felt such excitement that he worked with the speed of a whirlwind. The days sped by in eager preparation for the great event. Finally came the day to start.

To Agba, on that early morning of April, the road to Newmarket seemed never-ending. He was in a fever of expectancy. He wanted to break ranks, as Sham was urging him to do. He wanted to plunge ahead of Titus Twickerham on Galompus, the lead horse. But he must keep the pace set.

Behind him he could hear the light hoofbeats of Sham's three sons and the heavy cloppety-clop of the pack horses.

Perhaps if he took his eyes from the striped body jacket of Titus Twickerham and the stout rump of Galompus, the pace would not seem so slow! He tried to study the farms they passed, the tidy cottages with old men on the doorsteps and young men in the fields. He tried to count the long-necked geese in the four-storied carts they passed. He peered down the byways. He saw a shepherd and his dog driving a flock of sheep toward market. He even tried to imagine what the sheep were thinking of the passing horses.

But it was no use. New-mar-ket! New-mar-ket! The word kept dangling before him like a blade in the sun. New-mar-ket! New-mar-ket! He heard it in the rhythm of the hoofbeats, in the creak of cartwheels, in the song of the cuckoo. New-mar-ket!

They climbed a gentle rise. They passed through a toll gate. And then, suddenly, Newmarket Heath lay spread out before them. Agba gasped in dismay. It was not that Newmarket was less beautiful than he had expected. It was not that at all. He looked at the vast greenness of it. He smelled the fragrance of the turf. And instead of one racecourse, there were many. But what made a lump rise in Agba's throat was that everywhere, in all directions, exercise boys were galloping their horses. He shut his eyes, but he only saw them more clearly. The satin bodies of horses. Horses flying. Horses stretched out in the wind.

His mind raced back to what the Earl had told him only last evening. "You may walk your horse over the dips and rises," he had said kindly. "But do not gallop him. He is far more valuable than a running horse, Agba. He is the hope of Gog Magog."

And Mister Twickerham had added his own

word of caution. "If I c-c-c-catches ye galloping him, I'll trounce ye w-w-w-within an inch of yer life!"

At the time, Agba had readily agreed. It would be enough happiness, he had thought, to see Lath and Cade and Regulus run. Now he was not so sure. How he wanted Sham to run! To prove that he *was* King of the Wind!

The Earl's horses were always allowed several days in Newmarket to limber up before the day of the meeting. For Agba and Sham these days dragged. They were *in* Newmarket, but not of it. The Earl seemed too busy to pay any attention to them. His whole concern was in Lath, Cade, Regulus. He had not even told Agba where Sham was to be stationed when he watched his sons run.

Agba wished he and Sham had never come to Newmarket! He listened to the talk going on about him, sifting out the words that mattered.

"Regulus will run one heat over the Round Course on Thursday."

"Cade will run one heat over the Beacon Course on Friday."

"On Saturday, Lath will run one heat over the Caesarewitch Course for the honor and the glory of the Queen's Plate!"

After that, thought Agba, it will be over and done with. He would be glad to go back to Gog Magog. Then he and Sham could lose themselves for hours at a time in the upland pasture.

Monday, Tuesday passed. Wednesday came. All day the Earl and Mister Twickerham passed by Sham's tent as if they were unaware of his being there. Thursday came. Agba tried to busy himself shaking up the straw of Sham's bed, cleaning out his hooves, anointing his body with sheep's-foot oil. By midmorning he was doing the same tasks over and over, like a dog in a treadmill cage. His neck ached from looking up expectantly at every footfall. Perhaps the Earl would ask Sham to be the lead horse, to guide the nervous young fillies and colts to the starting post. There was still time. He might come.

The sun climbed higher and higher. The excitement all about them mounted. But Agba and Sham were isolated. No one came near them. They seemed more alone than when they were in the fen country.

Noon came. Regulus was led by Sham's stall on his way to the Round Course. Agba heard the saddling bell. He heard the winding of the trumpet. He heard the cry as if from a thousand throats,

"They're away!" Then the quickening music of hoofbeats. A few brief seconds, and they began fading, growing fainter and fainter until they were gone.

Agba was glad, of course, when he heard the cries of "Regulus! Regulus!" and knew that Sham's youngest son had won the two-year-old race. All the rest of the day he told himself how very glad he was. But there was a kind of hollowness in his gladness. Sham was unnoticed. Forgotten.

When Cade won the three-year-old race on the second day, Agba went right on sewing a strap that Sham had torn from his horsecloth. This was not news. He had known it all along. Did not Cade, like Regulus, have Sham's blood flowing in his veins? Was he not sired by the King of the Wind? Did he not have the white spot on his heel? With each question Agba's needle whipped in and out of the blanket, faster, faster.

A shadow suddenly fell across his work. He looked up into the twinkling gray eyes of the Earl of Godolphin.

"Agba!" cried the Earl with a boyish grin. "A great honor is come! The King and Queen of England will attend the final race meet tomorrow. And the Keeper of the Course has invited the Godolphin Arabian to stand at the finish post. Think on it, Agba! The King and Queen on one side. And directly opposite, the Godolphin Arabian!"

Agba was on his feet in an instant.

"And you, gentle Agba, will be up!" Then the Earl chuckled. "Though Twickerham insists upon two lead grooms to hold him. He does not trust Sham when the horses are off."

A group of the Earl's friends were coming toward him. The Earl lowered his voice and spoke quickly. "The amulets," he whispered, "do you still wear them about your neck?"

Agba took the silken bag from his neck and handed it to the Earl.

The Earl winked. "Hmm," he smiled. "If the amulets can prevent and cure the bite of a scorpion, they can give Lath wings."

He turned to go, then came back. "I do not need to tell you to curry the Godolphin Arabian," he smiled with his eyes. "Already his coat is the color of honey when held in a jar against the sunlight."

News of the King's and Queen's coming flew over the countryside. From Suffolk and Norfolk, from Hertford and Bedford, from nearly all the shires in England, the people came! Peers and lords and ladies in velvets and gold lace, yeomen in sturdy homespun, professors from Cambridge, gamekeepers with partridges in their pockets, moneylenders and Quakers, maltmen and saddlers and whipmakers and aldermen and squires and maids and housewives. They came on horseback. They came in coaches. They came afoot.

They spread themselves along Devil's Dyke where, long years ago, the Britons had dug a ditch to stem invasions. Now the dyke was overgrown with the finest turf in the kingdom. The people stood on it, sat on it, waiting for the sun to mark the middle of the day.

Within Sham's tent the very air seemed to crackle with excitement. The Earl of Godolphin himself was laying a purple saddlecloth on Sham's back, and fastening gold ornaments on his bridle and breastplate. Two grooms stood ready with silken lead ropes. They were dressed in the Earl's stable colors — scarlet silk body jackets and long scarlet stockings. What a contrast Agba made! His feet and legs were bare, and he wore his plain mantle. But he sat his horse with such pride that he might have worn ermine.

Now Sham was parading to the finish post. Agba kept his eyes forward. Yet he was aware of an undertone as of bees buzzing. The deep tones of men's voices. The grace notes of women. He caught wisps of talk.

"I prefers 'em lustier, stouter-limbed."

"Little as a cricket, hain't he?"

"He's the gold of the sun."

"Egad! Note the crest on him!"

"Lookit the artist, there, sketching a likeness o' 'im."

"That young man astride him — I knew him when he was just a little mite. My poor boy! I used to bake sugar tarts for him."

Agba turned his head very slightly, and from the sea of faces he picked out the plump, red-cheeked face and the shining eyes of Mistress Cockburn. A look of affectionate greeting flew between them.

Now there was a crash of drums and a flourish of trumpets as the Light Dragoons on matched horses swept into the race grounds. They were clearing a path for the royal party. The crowds fell back like thistles before the wind. Then shouts went up on all sides: "Long live the King! Long live the King!"

The coaches wheeled to a stop. Escorts rushed forward, followed by the Mayor of Newmarket and all the aldermen and squires. They bowed low before His Royal Majesty, George II, King of Great Britain and Ireland. The King was little in stature, but he strutted to the stand, his purple body coat flaring out behind him like the tail of a peacock.

Queen Caroline, tall as a pikestaff, swept along behind him. Her gown was corded and hooped with pearls, and she wore ropes of pearls about her neck, and her bonnet was bedecked with purple plumes.

Mincing along behind her came the princesses, Amelia and Caroline and Mary and Louisa, miniatures of their splendid mother. They were followed by lords and ladies in great number.

The cheering had scarcely died away when the entries for the race were led past the royal stand. Each of the horses was hooded and blanketed in the vivid colors of his own stable — red, yellow, purple, gray, orange.

Agba was dazzled by the sight. It was as if some sky giant had opened a jewel bag and tossed rubies, amethysts, sapphires, and moonstones onto the grass.

Quickly he spotted the scarlet sheet that enveloped Lath, though he could see only two pricked ears and the whisk of his tail.

184

Over in the royal stand the heads of the lords and ladies were bobbing this way and that, adjusting their field glasses. They seemed more interested in making out the crests on the blankets than in the quality of the legs and feet beneath them.

Agba's eyes gathered in the whole spectacle. He was glad that he had come. He had wanted so terribly to see Sham run. But now he knew that it was better this way. How could Sham compete with the youngsters of the turf? Especially when one of them was his own son?

Sham was alerted, waiting for a signal from Agba. Yet he stood still, obedient to Agba's wishes. It was better so. Defeat would have broken his heart. Now he was forever unbeaten. In his own mind and in Agba's he was still the wind beneath the sun. Neither horse nor gazelle could outrun him.

The saddle bell ended Agba's thoughts. His eyes flew to the starter, who was unfurling his red flag, sending his assistant a dozen yards down the track. He watched the trumpeter blowing on his trumpet, his face rounder than a goatsack.

Now the horses were parading to the starting post. They were drawing up in a line. Nervous as grasshoppers. Dancing. Side-stepping. Rearing.

185

Starting and being led back. Starting again. And again. And again.

The moment came. The starter dropped his red flag. "They're away!"

Not for one second did Agba need to hunt for Lath in that flying stream of horseflesh. He did not even look for the scarlet and white stripes of the jockey's body coat. His eyes were fixed on the littlest horse, the littlest horse that got away to a bad start!

The field was far out in front. The big horses were whipping down the steep slope to Devil's Dyke, skimming along the running gap, leaping up the opposite bank and across a long flat stretch. They were beginning to bunch, making narrow gaps. Lath was coming up from behind. He began filling in the gaps. He went through them. He was a blob of water color, trickling along the green turf between the other colors.

For a brief second the horses were hidden by a clump of hawthorn trees. Agba's knees tightened. He felt Sham quiver beneath him, saw white flecks of sweat come out on his neck. It was well the grooms were there to hold them both!

The horses were coming around the trees now.

The golden blob was still flowing between the other colors. It was flowing beyond them, flowing free!

In full stride, Lath was galloping down the dip and up the rise to the ending post. He was flying past it, leaving the "lusty" horses behind.

"The *little* horse wins!"

"Lath, an easy winner!"

"Lath, son of Godolphin Arabian, wins!"

People of all ages and all ranks clapped their hands and cheered in wild notes of triumph.

Agba never knew how he and Sham reached the royal stand. But suddenly, there they were. And the Earl of Godolphin was there too.

"I am pleased to give," Queen Caroline was saying in her sincere, straightforward manner, "I am pleased to give and bestow upon the Earl of Godolphin the Queen's Plate."

Everyone could see it was not a plate that she held in her hands at all. It was a purse. But only Agba and the Earl knew how much that purse would mean to the future of the horse in England. The Earl looked right between the plumes in the Queen's bonnet and found Agba's eyes for an instant. Then he fell to his knees and kissed the Queen's hand.

187

A hush fell over the heath. The Queen's words pinged sharp and clear, like the pearls that suddenly broke from her necklace and fell upon the floor of the stand. No one stooped to recover them, for the Queen was speaking.

"And what," she asked, as she fixed one of her own purple plumes in Sham's headstall, "what is the pedigree of this proud sire of three winning horses?"

Agba leaned forward in his saddle.

There was a pause while the Earl found the right words. "Your Majesty," he spoke slowly, thoughtfully, "his pedigree has been . . . has been lost. But perhaps it was so intended. His pedigree is written in his sons."

How the country people cheered! An unknown stallion wearing the royal purple! It was a fairy tale come true.

The princesses clapped their hands too. Even the King seemed pleased. He puffed out his chest and nodded to the Queen that the answer was good.

Agba swallowed. He felt a tear begin to trickle down his cheek. Quickly, before anyone noticed, he raised his hand to brush it away. His hand stopped. Why, he was growing a beard! He was a

188

man! Suddenly his mind flew back to Morocco. *My name is Agba. Ba means "father." I will be a father to you, Sham, and when I am grown I will ride you before the multitudes. And they will bow before you, and you will be King of the Wind. I promise it.*

He had kept his word!

For the first time in his life, he was glad he could not talk. Words would have spoiled everything. They were shells that cracked and blew away in the wind. He and Sham were alike. That was why they understood each other so deeply.

The Godolphin Arabian stood very still, his regal head lifted. An east wind was rising. He stretched out his nostrils to gather in the scent. It was laden with the fragrance of windflowers. Of what was he thinking? Was he rerunning the race of Lath? Was he rejoicing in the royal purple? Was he drawing a wood cart in the streets of Paris? Or just winging across the grassy downs in the shafts of the sun?

FATHER OF THE TURF

THE GODOLPHIN ARABIAN lived to a plentiful age. And when he died, at the age of twenty-nine, his body was buried at Gog Magog in a passage leading to his stable. Over his grave a tablet of solid granite was laid. There was no inscription on it. None at all. For the Earl of Godolphin did not need words carved on stone to remind him of the fire and spirit of the golden stallion from Morocco. He had only to look out upon his own meadows to see the living image of Sham in his colts and grand-colts. There were light bays and dark bays and chestnuts. But regardless of color, they all wore the high crest of the Godolphin Arabian.

"These are my knights of the wonderful crest," the Earl of Godolphin would say when visitors came to Gog Magog. "The blood of the Godolphin Arabian courses in their veins. You can trace it in the height of their crest. And you can trace it, too, in the underlying gold of their coats."

At Newmarket, however, men were not concerned with color or crest. What they were interested in was speed and stamina. And it was exactly these qualities that the descendants of the Godolphin Arabian inherited.

The names of Godolphin's offspring were on every tongue: Lath, Cade, Regulus, Babraham, Blank, Buffcoat, Match'em, Molly Longlegs, Whistlejacket, Weasel, Old England, Silverlocks, Dormouse.

Eclipse, Sham's great-grandson, was the pride of the kingdom. In his whole career he never ran except to win. He won eleven plates at Newmarket. "Eclipse first; the rest nowhere!" roared the crowds when Eclipse came sailing past the winning post.

It is a curious fact that today, two centuries later, the name of the Godolphin Arabian is found in the pedigree of almost every superior Thoroughbred. To him goes the title: Father of the Turf.

Would not the carter of Paris and the King's cook and the mistress of the Red Lion have laughed in scorn at the idea of Sham's attaining such fame? How they would have held their sides had anyone predicted that Man o' War, the greatest racer of his time, would owe his vitality to the fiery little horse from Morocco!

The Earl of Godolphin, however, would not have been surprised in the least. Perhaps he felt that some such honor would come to his horse. For when the Earl grew to be an old, old man he liked to take his visitors to Sham's grave. And when they asked why the tablet bore no marking, he would say, "I shall trouble you with a very short answer. It *needs* none. You see," he would smile, a faraway look in his eye, "the golden bay was tended all his life by a boy who could not speak. He left for Morocco the night that his horse died. Without any words at all he made me understand that his mission in life was fulfilled.

"So I have kept the tablet clean. It is for you and for me to write here our thoughts and tributes to the King of the Wind and the slim brown horseboy who loved him."

After the Earl's death, the Godolphin Arabian's name and the year of his death were inscribed on the tombstone. Time, however, is erasing the letters, as if in respect to the Earl's wishes.